Sea-Change

'Full fathom five thy father lies . . .'

From the very beginning in Tenerife it is obvious that the accidental drowning of Alex Hunter is not quite what it seems — but then nothing is what it seems in this story full of ambiguous questions.

Catherine Hunter, the beautiful and grieving (?) widow, her desolate schoolgirl daughter, her son David, who is by no means satisfied with the official explanation of his father's death . . . are they real, or are they inventions living an extraordinary charade? And unaware of the fact?

Alex Hunter's friend and business partner, handsome Patrick MacAlistair, flies out to Tenerife to deal with the formalities (and deals with the Guardia Civil, somewhat curiously, in the process). But why does he lie to the dead man's family? Who are the faceless men five thousand miles away following his every move? Why does he identify the body of a perfect stranger as being that of his friend?

The questions asked on the sunny island in the Atlantic are answered in a stuffy room behind a London art gallery, and reach a deadly conclusion in the streets of Vienna during a snowstorm. Who really 'suffers a sea-change'? Dead Alex Hunter, his wife, his son, his best friend? Or all four of them?

PHILIP LORAINE

Sea-Change

COLLINS, ST JAMES'S PLACE, LONDON

William Collins Sons & Co. Ltd
London · Glasgow · Sydney · Auckland
Toronto · Johannesburg

First published 1982
© Philip Loraine 1982

British Library Cataloguing in Publication Data

Loraine, Philip
Sea-change. — (The Crime Club).
I. Title
823'.914 [F]   PR6062.067

ISBN 0-00-231725-7

Photoset in Compugraphic Baskerville
Printed in Great Britain by
T. J. Press (Padstow) Ltd

Full fathom five thy father lies;
Of his bones are coral made;
Those are pearls which were his eyes;
Nothing of him that doth fade,
But doth suffer a sea-change
Into something rich and strange.
Sea-nymphs hourly ring his knell:
                    Ding-dong.
Hark! Now I hear them—Ding-dong bell.

The Tempest

PART ONE

TENERIFE

'Full fathom five thy father lies . . .'

1

'Five-nine-seven-nine.'

'Peter here. Sorry I was out when you . . .'

'Listen—did you send Joanna to Tenerife?'

'This morning.'

'Arriving when?'

'Plane got in at ten-fifteen.'

'How long does it take from the airport to this place?'

'Las Rocas. Joanna couldn't have made it until about . . . eleven o'clock their time, at the earliest.'

'Well, Alex Hunter's dead—*ten* o'clock their time. Drowned.'

'Drowned!'

'Right. Mrs Hunter's sent for MacAlistair, husband's partner, best friend, etcetera.'

'Specially etcetera.'

'Here's what you do. Ready?'

'Go ahead.'

'I want to know exactly what happened—accident, suicide or murder—if murder, who did it and why?—definite verification of death, the body hasn't turned up yet—Hunter's movements since he got to the island—any long-distance telephone calls immediately prior to his death. Follow me?'

'I certainly do. What about MacAlistair?'

'Treat him as a risk, and I mean a risk. Hunter's son and daughter are there, could be the best source of information, properly handled.'

'And the Spaniards?'

'They've got to be kept out of it.'

'Not so easy.'

'We're not in an easy racket, didn't you know?'

'Do you want Joanna to come back?'

'No. Tell her to stay put, low profile. And, Peter, I'm in the hot seat, Lorenz wants answers by Friday.'

'*Friday*!'

'Right. Move it!'

2

David Hunter was sitting on a rock, gazing at the patch of Atlantic Ocean into which his father had disappeared, when the question of the reading glasses first came creeping up on him: so small a question to have such enormous, indeed disastrous, consequences.

A kind of jittery calm possessed him; he recognized it from his only experience of a road-accident; shock had overtaken him long afterwards, he supposed that the same thing was going to happen now. In the meantime death, as demonstrated by his first personal encounter with it, seemed oddly inconclusive considering how final it was supposed to be: perhaps because his father's body was still missing.

A black-haired, grey-eyed, sturdy young man of nineteen (his subject was Agrobiology, 'the science of plant growth and nutrition in relation to agriculture'), he was ashamed of himself because he was feeling only this tense hiatus and not a jot of proper grief as he understood it. Moreover, his mother seemed to be suffering the same

affliction; their conversations were stilted and per-
functory, as if they'd just been introduced at a noisy party
and had nothing particular in common: when all the time
they had everything in common, including this gigantic
experience, the death of a man whom they had both
loved.

David could almost, but not quite, envy his sister Anne,
who was refusing to eat and who showed, whenever she
opened her bedroom door, the tear-bloated face of
conventional mourning; he had not known that she
possessed such practical emotional fluency, Latin in its
abandonment. He himself took after their mother who
came of a British army family not given to weeping and
breast-beating; meeting her eye across Annie's bowed and
sniffling head, he almost felt that they were saying to each
other, as generations of her family certainly would have
said, 'Really, these foreigners!'

Analytical by nature as well as by training, he had
examined what he felt to be his own lack of decent grief
and had concluded that it stemmed directly from the fact
that he could accept neither of the possible causes of
his father's death, accident and suicide. The police,
represented by an unusually dapper officer of the
Guardia Civil, seemed to have settled for accident. Mrs
Hunter concurred. Annie, words failing her, wept afresh.
Only David disagreed; accident made no sense whatever;
his father had been a strong swimmer; more than once
they had together braved the notorious ebbing tide off
Punto del Barranco, finding it a lot less powerful than its
reputation, returning no more than pleasurably breath-
less to bake themselves on these flat rocks before climbing
up to the cantina at the end of the village street for a
beer.

But on the other hand suicide was even more absurd;
everything about his father, character, humour, success,
attitude to life, contradicted the idea. In any case suicide

surely implied farewell notes, and there had been no
farewell notes, unless . . .

He looked up at the villa, already in shadow because it
faced south-east. His mother's figure, wearing some pale
garment, moved across the terrace like an owl at dusk.
His heart went out to her, but at the same time he knew
that had she received a farewell note she wouldn't
necessarily reveal the fact, to her son or to the police, if
she considered the contents unacceptable. Not that he
had any particular reason to suppose that his parents'
relationship encompassed unacceptables, though he had
often wondered about his mother's true reaction to his
father's frequent and sometimes interminable absences.
Was it one of the things a wife settled for if she expected
the male to go out into the world and provide? The
answer lay within the adult precinct which he had not yet
properly entered: as did the ramifications of Artifax Ltd
(and Inc.), the successful business which Alex Hunter had
run with his American partner, Patrick MacAlistair.

David shook his head impatiently, and looked down at
the exact spot where, coming to join his father for the
morning swim, he had found the neat pile of belongings:
suntan oil, sunglasses, *The Ides of March* in paperback,
espadrilles, towel, jeans, and shirt with 5000 pesetas in
the pocket; the watch, being a Rolex, stayed on the wrist.
And it was at this moment that the fatal thought pounced
on him: why sunglasses and not the glasses which his
father always used for reading? Why a book and nothing
through which to see it? Nobody went for a swim in their
reading glasses, and even supposing that some acquisitive
local had thought them worth stealing—unlikely—he
would hardly have overlooked the 5000 pesetas clearly
visible in the shirt pocket. Then where were they?

Pondering this question, he turned and began to climb
the rough path towards the villa, while behind him the sun,
having turned a bloody red, foundered into the Atlantic.

Of course it was entirely possible that his father had forgotten the glasses, giving Mr Thornton Wilder a miss on this particular morning, and even if this was so their absence pointed to an interesting hypothesis: his lack of decent grief was not caused by some emotional failing, as he had begun to fear, it was based on an analysable gap between cause and effect. Research into many complicated subjects, such as Environmental Biology, had shown him that accepted authorities were apt to leap nimbly over such gaps only when their source-material was inadequate; the source-material regarding his father's death was exactly that, inadequate, and he was pleased that his academic training could recognize the fact.

At this point, toiling up the steep hillside between banana groves and stony fields inset with brilliant tomatoes, he came to an abrupt halt, gazing blankly at Mount Tiede which had all the time been sliding slowly into view with his own slow ascent; the peak still caught the last high sunlight, and pink clouds were mimicking the volcanic smoke of long ago.

Concentrated upon the casting out of accident and suicide, he had not realized until this moment that their elimination would leave a vacuum and that this would automatically be filled by the only other possibility. But it was inconceivable that anyone could have wanted to murder his father!

3

Las Rocas, the nearest town to the villa temporarily occupied by the Hunter family, was too small to warrant its own detachment of the Guardia Civil. They operated out of Santa Cruz, the island's capital. Here, in a dusty

office lined with massive legal treatises, most of them
obsolete, dominated by a bust of Cervantes, no one knew
why, Lieutenant Dominguez of the Guardia faced Señor
Landero, a magistrate. Dominguez, whom David Hunter
had considered dapper, was tall for a Spaniard, sleek,
mustachioed, admired by ladies; the magistrate was
desiccated, balding, dusty like his office. He said, in a
desiccated voice, 'Are they people of importance?'

It was a vital question, both men knew it, and
Dominguez answered carefully in consequence. If a
packaged tourist from, say, Manchester was so foolish as
to be swept out to sea and drowned, the formalities would
be set in motion and, with no more than a gentle push
from Señor Landero and Lieutenant Dominguez, would
trundle away down the well-worn slope of bureaucratic
routine, barely interrupting their respective siestas; if the
visitor was important, as a private villa well off the tourist
track implied, ah then . . .

'The house belongs to the family Villa de Sangre,' said
the officer without emphasis.

'Rich.' The statement was glum.

'Yes. They lend it to the Hunters.'

The magistrate's heart sank. Lending indicated
familiarity with this prestigious Spanish name. Wasn't
one of them in politics, even in government?

'Señor Hunter was a businessman. English. Resident in
London.'

'What business?'

Lieutenant Dominguez knew that the magistrate was
trying to catch him out in dereliction of his duty; it was an
old game, there was no love lost between them. Señor
Landero, like many another in Santa Cruz, envied the
policeman his youth, his dashing good looks, and the fact
that he had evaded marriage, preferring regular visits
to the house of Dolores Calvo. The truth was that
Dominguez didn't actually *like* women, except in the

horizontal position, and had no intention of allowing one to destroy his well-ordered life with demands and questions and, worst of all, children. Señor Landero, on the other hand, possessed a stringy wife, two sons who declined to work, and two daughters without suitors.

For these reasons he had demanded 'What business?' tetchily, and for these reasons the policeman decided to repay the old scorpion by giving him a full answer: 'It is called Artifax and is concerned with the import and export of foreign goods for the home—large items such as beds, sofas, tables, chairs, garden furniture, smaller items such as baskets, boxes, pictures, statuary, lamps, mirrors, rugs, cushions, ceramics, glassware, many kinds of—'

'Yes, yes.' The magistrate knew that he had brought this boring recital upon himself.

'He had,' Dominguez added slyly, 'offices in London and Paris, also in the USA, New York and Houston.'

The magistrate's sinking heart came to rest, as the policeman had known it would, in his dyspeptic old stomach. London, Paris, New York, Houston! Las Rocas was an insignificant village at the very edge of the Western world; Señor Landero himself had only been there half a dozen times, Lieutenant Dominguez hardly more often; why must these foreigners bother with it? Sun was the answer, of course; in winter they came sweeping down from the frozen North, throwing off their thermal underwear, to prostrate themselves on Tenerife's rare beaches and beside her many swimming-pools, the rocks invariably being too sharp because of their volcanic origin. Very few of the tourists were well-to-do, but unfortunately it seemed that this man Hunter was one of them.

'They have stayed at the villa once before,' the policeman continued. 'The wife is perhaps forty, aristocratic, attractive. There are two children, a boy and a girl in their teens.'

'Lovers?'

'Not that I know of. Not resident.'

'Must we then deal with the son, a boy?'

'No. The husband's partner, an American, Señor Patrick MacAlistair—' Spanish made mincemeat of this name—'arrives tonight or tomorrow.'

The magistrate nodded. A partner, a businessman, an American, that was good. 'You will talk with this Señor . . . Patrick.'

The policeman nodded.

'The body has not yet reappeared.'

'No. The tide was going out, you know what that means. He may have been washed up this side of Punto de Teno; if so, nobody will find him. Alternatively . . .'

Senor Landero sighed; both knew that the ebbing tide could weave concentric circles round the southern tip of the island, running in opposite directions. 'He might,' the magistrate said, 'just as well turn up along the Costa del Silencio.' The thought of this barren coast, populated only by seabirds and lizards and sun-crazed Germans, filled both men with gloom.

'I hope for your sake,' added Señor Landero, giving the younger man an acid glance, 'that is to say, in view of your present position, that a body will appear.'

Dominguez, smoothing the elegant moustache with a manicured index finger, knew that this was a reference to his expected promotion. He also noted that his superior had said 'a body' not 'the body'.

4

During dinner, at which they discussed only the practical problems caused by Alex Hunter's death, David realized that he was trapped in a powerful process of reassessment.

He was actually sitting there over his chicken salad reassessing his mother as if she were indeed some stranger encountered at a party. It had been the same with his sister when they had both tried to prise her out of her bedroom to partake of sustenance and sympathy. Mercifully, in David's opinion, she had refused both.

Noting the dark smudges under Catherine Hunter's fine grey eyes, which he had inherited, and the unusually firm set of the lips, her son found himself wondering whether she was not after all a highly emotional person who had been pressed like a once-succulent flower between the disciplinary boards of her upbringing. The simile came to him naturally, since his earliest involvement with botany had taken the form of pressing and drying various plants for later identification.

David was fond of his Matheson grandparents (the Hunter ones were in Australia) and didn't in the least mind being pressed and commanded by the General, understanding that it was hard for the old boy, having commanded all his life, to find that the garrison had dwindled to a mere village, Little Athelston in Wiltshire, scene of his retirement. But grandsons could escape, daughters could not.

When David came to think of it, which he did over melon and grapes, he had never heard his mother complain about her military upbringing; on the whole she seemed to have found the discipline bearable and the vagrancy stimulating; her memories were extrovert and jolly: parties, tennis, riding, platoons of handsome young officers in uniform. But it was significant that the handsome young officer she had chosen to marry didn't like the army at all and had left it as soon as possible. This must have been a shock for the grandparents, but naturally they had never voiced it, except perhaps in private. They loved their son-in-law and would be stricken by the news of his death, while at the same time expecting their daughter to 'bear up', 'take it on the chin', etcetera: which, witness the smudged eyes and the tight lips, their daughter was doing. But what, her own son wondered over his coffee, was she really thinking and feeling?

Such questions were the reverse side of reassessment; they hadn't even existed this morning when his father had announced that he was going down to the rocks for a swim. Or perhaps they had existed, and David Hunter, intent on himself, his studies, his future, hadn't been aware of them.

Since this morning, everything had acquired new depths; for instance he had always known that his mother was a presentable woman, but now he realized, watching her as she stood by the window, herself watching the beam of the distant lighthouse on Punta de la Rasoa, that she was beautiful. The discovery shocked and unsettled him; he was half afraid of what he might find out next.

She said, 'Of course there *would* be a strike!' She was referring to the non-arrival of Patrick MacAlistair, who was unable to reach them until the following morning.

David said, 'I could probably have managed — the formalities. My Spanish isn't *that* bad.'

Catherine Hunter smiled, and her son thought that to her, to the whole world perhaps, he was little more than a boy. As if aware of the thought and unwilling to hurt his pride, she added, 'But then there's the business, you see. Patrick's the only person who understands that.'

'Do you like him?' The question surprised David even as he asked it.

Surprised her too. 'Like him? Well . . .' She was troubled, another mystery, and turned away, again looking at the beam of the lighthouse. 'I've never thought about it really; somehow he . . . he's always been there, hasn't he?'

Yes, Patrick MacAlistair had always been there. David

wondered what he was going to find in *him* which hadn't existed before the morning swim.

But he loved his mother and understood her, to a certain extent (to what extent? he hadn't even realized that she was a beautiful woman until five minutes ago!) and so said, 'Are you . . . all right?'

'All right?' She shrugged. 'I don't know. I feel . . . numb. At breakfast he was here and I was angry with him for cutting short his holiday because of business . . .'

'I didn't know about that.'

'He said he might miss the last week and go to New York. And I was . . . oh, boring and spiteful.'

So she *did* care about the endless business trips: five months once!

'And then, suddenly, he isn't here any more, and we never even finished the conversation, I never said I was sorry.' She shrugged again, and sighed. 'Well, nothing in life is tidy, it's always a bit of a mess.'

Had they ever talked like this together before? No, not quite like this. And why had he asked that question anyway? Of course they all liked Patrick MacAlistair. Didn't they?

Uncertainly he said, 'I thought it was going to, you know, hit me later, but now . . .'

'Oh, it'll hit *me* all right. Not in the street, I hope.'

He crossed to the window, put an arm around her shoulder, hugged her. 'We'll get by.'

She studied his face intently, but not, he thought, with quite the old acceptance of him as her little boy. Was she reassessing too? 'Yes, we'll get by. You're a great help to me, Davey, but I knew you would be. So did your father.'

'He did?'

'Why the surprise?'

'It's just . . . He didn't really know me all that well. I mean, being away so much.'

The grey eyes continued to examine him, but they were

guarded now. And it was in a guarded, more parental voice that she said, 'You might try to get some sense into Annie on your way to bed. Tell her there's food in the fridge, I've a feeling she'll emerge like a wounded animal once we're out of the way.

His sister's bedroom door was still locked but she said, 'Hang on a sec!' and after a pause (during which she did what, for heaven's sake? combed her hair? hid her rosary? dressed?) she allowed him to enter. The tears seemed to have abated, giving way to a mournful solemnity which David found irritating—but why? wasn't she the only one of them who was behaving correctly? Without a doubt *she* thought so; her stare was that of a missionary despairing of a soul.

Anne Hunter was fifteen. She had inherited her father's features, his brown hair and eyes, all seeming to require male hormones to bring out the best in them. She could make herself reasonably pretty when she took the trouble, but at the moment she looked a mess because she wanted to look a mess: pale face with red nose peering from lank untidy hair. David, seeing his reflection beyond her, in the mirror over the dressing-table, could well appreciate her feelings towards him; grey-eyed, black-haired, tanned from long days in the sun, he not only seemed to belong to another family but gave the impression of being insensitive and unharrowed; again he was ashamed of his lack of visible grief.

When he told her about the chicken salad in the refrigerator she glanced away and said, 'Food!' No good pretending that this didn't increase his irritation. The inference was: I suppose you and mother have been stuffing yourselves—well, it takes all sorts!

He tried. 'Annie, it's happened, we're going to have to live with it.'

'Oh, go away!'

'Ma's taking it very well, I don't see why you can't . . .'

'She never loved him, that's why.'

'Don't be such a twit!'

'She didn't.'

'They had us.'

'Anybody, *everybody* has kids!' With scorn.

So then he lost his temper and said, 'You really are selfish, aren't you? Only Anne has feelings, only Anne gets hurt . . .'

She began to cry again. 'If . . . if we'd loved him more, he . . . he wouldn't have done it.'

David had himself progressed so far beyond the idea of suicide that he was quite taken aback by this ingenuous simplicity. Misreading his expression she said, 'Well, you don't think it was an *accident*, surely? He was a fantastic swimmer.'

'No. And I don't think it was suicide either, suicides leave notes.' For a moment he thought that she was going to produce just such a note and wave it under his nose; she merely said, 'Not always.'

'He was forty-four, successful, quite rich, happy . . .'

'Happy? How do you know?'

'I just think he was.'

'Hah!' This of course could mean anything and probably meant nothing. He excused his sister by recalling that she had loved her father very much, perhaps too much, like many another daughter; also, fifteen was not the happiest of ages for a girl who wasn't sure whether she was more interested in God or boys. He tried to be gentle. 'It could have been an accident, Annie. Cramp, even a heart attack.'

Her look was pitying.

'The thing is we . . . we have to *accept* that he's dead.'

'To make life easier for ourselves, I suppose!'

He knew that if he stayed another minute he would slap her, so he said, 'Good night, love. Don't forget the food if you feel like it.' At the door he turned and, thinking that the thought might cheer her, added, 'Patrick will be here tomorrow.'

With a venom which was shockingly uncharacter-istic — of her Christian aspect in particular — his sister said, 'And fuck him too!'

5

'Five-nine-seven-nine.'

'Peter here. Sorry if I woke you — you said any time.'

'I meant any time.'

'In the end I sent Morales and Acton.' The man in the telephone kiosk was slim, trim, with prematurely white hair and a darker moustache; he had reached the age at which the hair no longer made him look younger; only the percipient would have detected a faint Irish brogue. 'They both speak good Spanish. Well, Morales *is* Spanish.'

'Wait! I'm not alone.' The other man was fat, Italianate, always seeming to be in need of a shave even when he'd just had one. In spite of his bulk he slipped out of the bed quickly, deftly, pressed a 'hold' button on the phone, replaced the receiver, and went out of the room, pendulously naked.

The girl in the bed watched him without interest. When he lifted the receiver in the living-room the 'hold' button in the bedroom popped up automatically, dis-connecting the phone beside the bed. He said, 'Go on!'

'They arrived a couple of hours ago, just called me. They're at a place called Playa de las Americas, not too far from Hunter's villa. Kind of motel, bungalows, sounds right.'

'How's this being relayed to you?'

'Open — word-code. The lines are terrible anyway, and if you want answers by Friday . . .'

'How's Joanna?'

'Fine. Staying at a hotel in the town, Las Rocas.'

'Go on.'

'The body still hasn't turned up. Everybody takes accident for granted, he was swimming in a pretty dangerous place. The policeman in charge is called Dominguez; said to be intelligent and ambitious.'

'What do your boys plan to do?'

'Morales is moving in first thing tomorrow.'

'Remember they don't know MacAlistair. Warn them!'

'MacAlistair won't even be there, he's been held up by the strike.'

'Lucky.'

'Gives us a pretty free hand.'

'Gives *you* a pretty free hand, Peter, it's your baby.'

The white-haired young man in the telephone kiosk began to sweat suddenly, even though it was a cold night; he wiped the moisture from face and moustache with a scarlet, white-dotted handkerchief, one of his affectations. The fat voice said, 'Okay, go on. What's Morales's line?'

6

David Hunter remembered his father's reading glasses in the middle of a restless night. He even got out of bed and went downstairs to look for them. The search proved fruitless, but there were signs of his bereaved sister having abandoned her fast. Typically, she had eaten very little chicken salad, flattening what was left on to the dish so that it appeared untouched. Manic reassessment commanded him to look in the bread-bin; several healthy slices had been cut from her favourite wholemeal loaf. He resisted an urge to take the rest of the loaf and the salad and dump them outside her bedroom door, or, if it was unlocked, on top of her.

He could not have said why the matter of the missing glasses obsessed him; he was no longer interested in analysis, he simply felt compelled to find them. On his way back to bed he noticed a pale line of light under his mother's door, and thought that he heard . . . Yes, she was weeping quietly. Everything Matheson within him said, 'Leave her alone, don't intrude on private grief!' but something else made him open the door.

Catherine Hunter buried her face in the pillows, but when she felt him sit on the edge of the large bed she put out a hand blindly and he took it, surprised by the strength of her grip. After a moment she said, 'Don't . . . don't pander to me — I'm not crying . . . for the right reasons.'

The honesty touched his heart, and presumably illuminated his mind, because he heard himself saying, 'I don't suppose many people cry for the person who's actually dead. I mean, look at Annie — she's crying for Anne Hunter, no one else.'

His mother turned her head and stared at him, obviously surprised by this human perspicacity in her academic son who, only yesterday morning, had lectured her sternly on the growing behaviour of plant pathogens.

They sat for a time in silence; then she said, 'I'm all right now. Go back to bed, my dear, it must be nearly dawn.' He went back to bed and quickly fell asleep, dreaming that he had found the reading glasses hidden under Anne's pillow.

In the morning, he waited until his mother, looking frail and disoriented from lack of sleep, had gone downstairs for a cup of coffee, and as soon as he heard her talking to Paquita, the maid, he went into her bedroom again and continued the search. He had just finished with his father's sock drawer where the glasses were sometimes kept—he'd been sent to fetch them on many occasions—when Catherine Hunter called out, 'Davey, where are you?'

He managed to reach the middle of the landing by the time her head appeared on the staircase. 'Darling, there's someone from the insurance company . . .'

Pleased that she needed his help, he followed her downstairs and found a sallow apologetic young man with black curly hair standing in the hall, which always reminded him, with its overwrought iron, whorled plaster walls and black wooden furniture, of a bad stage set; even the palm outside the window and the brilliant sea beyond seemed ineptly painted, too bright. He had never met the prestigious Villa de Sangre family, business associates of his father, but in happier days he and Annie had exchanged awful jokes about bloody villas.

Catherine Hunter said, 'Señor . . .'

'Serrano.'

'This is my son, David.'

The young man bowed. He wore a crumpled pale grey suit with a black tie, and carried a worn document case; his dark eyebrows all but met in the middle, giving him a permanently worried expression. He said, 'I again apologize for intruding on your grief.'

'Not at all, Señor Serrano, it's your job.' Very much the General's daughter.

'My superior in Santa Cruz thought that as a result of this terrible experience you might wish to return to England as soon as possible. He felt we might be blamed by the London Office for not having, as it were, settled certain points . . .' His English was excellent but inclined to prolixity. Mrs Hunter rescued him by saying, 'I quite understand.' She gestured towards the living-room where the morning sunlight was painfully brilliant. Lowering a blind, David said, 'I didn't know Father carried insurance.'

'Oh yes, dear — Something Amalgamated.'

'West London Amalgamated,' said Señor Serrano, accepting the chair she indicated, putting his document case on his knees, producing from it a notebook. 'Much,' he added, 'must depend upon the medical evidence, but I assure you, señora, that we shall do all in our power to see that you receive your due recompense.'

'Thank you.' Catherine Hunter stared out of the window at the blazing blue sky which would presently grow colourless as the sun climbed into it. David noticed with a pang of pity how washed out she looked: literally, like a water-colour drawing which had faded to the original pencil. The dark smudges under the direct grey eyes were darker today. Perhaps to save the young man further embarrassment she said, 'But the evidence itself must depend on . . . on his body being found.'

Señor Serrano made the usual remarks about tides and currents, and added, 'That, señora, is why it's important for us to know certain things concerning the state of mind of your husband — excuse me, your late husband — prior to the tragedy. Would you say that he has been unusually nervous or upset these past few days?'

David said, 'No, not at all, he was fine.'

'You are quite sure, señor? No worries about his business in these hard times?'

'Funnily enough,' said Mrs Hunter, 'his business was booming. Doing very well. People are still spending money on their homes.'

'He did not receive any telephone calls, business calls perhaps, which might have caused him . . .'

'He didn't commit suicide, if that's what you mean.' She looked at her son as she spoke. David said, 'I agree. He wasn't . . . I mean, if you'd known him . . .'

At this point Anne walked into the room wearing her

nun's face. 'Good morning, Mother, I hope you don't mind me being here.'

'Darling, of course not, I'm so pleased you . . .'

Anne cut this short by turning her back and saying to Señor Serrano, 'My father did receive a telephone call—two telephone calls. One on Sunday night, that's the night before he . . .' She ended on a gulp.

David's surprise contended with his distaste, and won. Their mother said, 'Anne, are you sure?'

'You'd both gone to bed.' She managed to make even this sound like moral condemnation. 'I hadn't been lying in the sun all day so I wasn't tired.'

David, glancing at Señor Serrano, caught what could only have been a glint of satisfaction in the lustrous black eyes; hastily concealed. In spite of his protestations to the contrary there seemed little doubt that West London Amalgamated, like any other insurance company, was intent on making sure that Señora Hunter received nothing approaching her 'due recompense'. 'And the second call, señorita?'

'It was . . . It was only an hour before he . . . went down to the rocks.'

Her mother and her brother were staring at her, and in both pairs of eyes, so alike, she could read an old family scepticism. It was indeed true that long ago when she was young—well, two years ago when she was thirteen—she had been given to romanticizing; but that was before God, in the shape of Miss Taggart, one of her teachers and a devout Catholic, had entered her life and transformed it.

Señor Serrano said, 'Only an hour before he . . .'

'Yes.' And to her mother: 'It's true. You and Davey were out shopping.'

Certainly they had been out shopping.

'And I . . . I heard.'

Señor Serrano nodded and made a note. 'But that is

most interesting, señorita.'

'I was in the next room. Of course I didn't actually *listen*.'

'Naturally not.'

David glanced at his mother; both of them looked away hastily. So this, he was thinking, was the reason for his sibling's certainty regarding suicide: not by any means as half-baked as he had suspected. But why hadn't she told the police? He said it aloud: 'Why didn't you say anything to that policeman?'

'I didn't like him.' The non sequitur was pronounced with such aplomb that it almost made sense. 'And he *wanted* it to be an accident anyway.' Like many an obvious truth, this caused a small silence; broken by Señor Serrano: 'Señorita, was your father disturbed by the second telephone conversation—yesterday morning?'

'Well . . . yes, he was. He didn't even seem to hear me when I spoke to him. Then he went out. And then he came back and said he was sorry, and kissed me—for no reason really. He was . . . strange.' She looked at her mother and gaping brother again, not far from tears. 'He *was!*'

Señor Serrano sighed and turned to Catherine Hunter. 'You are still of the opinion, señora, that it was an accident?'

A pause; then, 'I don't think it was suicide.'

Anne looked at the ceiling and said, 'Only because you get more money that way.'

'*Anne!*' And from David at the same instant, '*Oh, for Christ's sake!*'

The girl looked down. She was crying again, messily. 'I'm sorry, I have to say what I think is true.'

David had never admired his mother's Matheson qualities more than at this moment. She got up and put her arms around her frightful female child; more extraordinarily, but women *were* extraordinary, Anne let out a gasp and hugged her mother tightly. Señor Serrano said, 'I am so sorry, so sorry. I must return at another time, I am clumsy . . .'

'No, no.' Mrs Hunter was smoothing her daughter's lank hair; she had even found a pretty handkerchief and was holding it to the pink nose as if that appendage belonged to a blubbering baby. David watched, appalled and fascinated. His mother continued, 'Ask your questions now; better to get it over with.'

'Perhaps the señorita wishes to retire.'

The señorita shook her head, gave her mother a wan but sincerely grateful smile, and turned to the window to recover her composure.

'I am desolated, señora, I lack all tactfulness.'

'Please — continue. We've already had most of these questions from the police.'

'Well then . . . I hate to ask, but do you have any reason to believe that your husband had enemies?'

'I would have said not, he was a kind, good man. But in business . . .' She shrugged. David knew instinctively that she was thinking of the many prolonged absences. He said, 'Mr MacAlistair, my father's partner, will be here some time this morning. He naturally knows all about that side of my father's life.'

'I think,' his mother added, 'that you can discount murder, if that's what you're talking about.'

'I apologize. I was told to ask all relevant questions.' The black brows were now drawn so tightly together that they made a single straight line across the sallow fore-head. 'I must therefore enquire, señorita — ' he glanced at Anne's slender back — 'if you know *who* telephoned your father yesterday morning, an hour before his death?'

Anne turned. David realized that he now felt genuinely sorry for her. In addition to the conscience and the inculcated sense of duty, which he shared, the poor girl was driven by all kinds of religious urges of which he was

mercifully ignorant. He could see that these were forcing
her to answer whether she wanted to or not. She said,
'Well, he didn't mention any name . . .' So much for her
being in the next room but, of course, not listening! 'I
thought . . . I mean, I think . . . I'm pretty sure it was
Patrick MacAlistair.'

'For what reason are you sure, señorita?'

'Because I've heard him talking to Patrick dozens of
times and, well, that's who it sounded like.'

Señor Serrano nodded and made another note. David
could see that his mother had had enough; he cleared his
throat, wondering how one terminated this kind of conversation; but Señor Serrano forestalled him: 'I have
asked too much, I beg to be forgiven.'

Catherine Hunter smiled. They stood up. Señor
Serrano repeated his assurances concerning the
charitable intentions of West London Amalgamated, and
then David escorted him to his car, the usual well-worn
Seat. The women out of earshot, man to man as it were,
the Spaniard said, 'Your father has been here, at the
villa, most of the time since you came on holiday, señor?'

'Yes. Apart from the odd shopping expedition to Las
Rocas. One picnic on Tiede.'

'No visits to Puerto or Santa Cruz?'

'None.'

Señor Serrano was studying his face. It struck David
that the moist black eyes under the single eyebrow were
noticably more acute than he had supposed; even as he
thought it, thick lashes again concealed them. 'I must
perhaps speak with this Señor . . . your father's partner.'

'MacAlistair. Patrick MacAlistair.'

'If possible I will do so without troubling your mother.
At what time did you say that Señor Mac . . . Alistair
arrives?'

'I didn't. About eleven-thirty.'

'Eleven-thirty at the airport?'

'Yes.' David was mistaken in this; it was a mistake which was to have consequences.

'I thank you, señor, you have all been most kind, most . . . direct. I like very much the English.' With which he climbed into his car and rattled away.

Returning to the villa, David found Anne tucking into coffee and the delicious rolls which Paquita brought from the village. Scrubbed and shiny-faced for her role of Nun, she seemed about ten years old. The look which she and their mother flashed at him was both conspiratorial and loving: women welcoming the male, with reservations. As a dedicated, if erratic, chess-player he had known occasions when somebody had nudged the board by mistake, shifting the pieces a little; though both players invariably said that they knew exactly how each had been placed, there was always a nagging feeling that somehow, somewhere, something had changed. So it was with life now; the death of Alex Hunter had jolted the board and nothing was quite what it had been before.

David felt excluded and insecure; he was tempted to throw a spanner in the womanly works by announcing that he was going down to the rocks for a swim, but realized just in time that though the furore would be satisfying it would lead to his mother forbidding him to do any such thing; and he, being a Matheson, would abide by his word. Whereas if he kept silent, womanly logic would assume that he couldn't possibly be so stupid as to contemplate swimming less than twenty-four hours after his father had been drowned in that very place. Stupid or not, this was what he intended to do; indeed *had* to do.

7

Señor Serrano, whose real name was Jake Morales (he had been christened Jesus but had dropped that for obvious reasons when he began to work with Anglo-Saxons) stopped the rented Seat at a roadside café, ordered a glass of fresh orange juice, and asked if he could use the telephone. This, as he knew from prior reconnaissance, was at the end of a passage and reasonably private; all the same, he intended to take no risks, he wasn't paid to take risks.

A woman's voice answered, and he said in his perfect Spanish, 'Señora, may I speak to an English friend, Señor Brown, who is waiting for my call at your establishment?'

After a pause his colleague, Colin Acton, picked up the receiver: 'Hello, Johnny, how's tricks?'

'Pretty good. You?'

'I'm fine. Nice view from here.' Since Acton was in the cantina at which Alex Hunter and his son had often taken a beer together after their swim, the view in question embraced, in one direction, the villa itself, and in the other a shaly cliff which hid the flat rocks where they had been in the habit of sunning themselves. Much of the steep path connecting the two was also visible; down this, not five minutes before the telephone call, Acton had seen David Hunter picking his way, deep in thought. In fact, David had been searching the path for some sign of his father's glasses, but from a distance scrutiny looks much like cogitation. He had, incidentally, not found a trace of them.

Acton was a thickset, fair young man who wore gold-rimmed glasses because he knew that they minimized a certain bully-boy truculence in his looks and manner; he said, 'How did all that go?'

'I had a nice talk with our friends.'

'Good.'

'They told me six or seven things I wanted to know.'

Acton glanced at a handwritten list on the bar beside the telephone, and put a tick against numbers six and seven.

'They also told me that Mr Jennings is arriving at the airport at eleven-thirty.'

'So he couldn't get *here* before twelve-fifteen, twelve-thirty, right?'

'Make it twelve, to be safe.'

'Leaves me time for a swim, doesn't it?'

'Better not swim alone; a chap was drowned yesterday.'

'I won't be alone. Young Martin's down there now.'

'Good. You might learn a thing or two, possibly three.'

Acton put a cross against numbers one and two on his list, and a questionmark against three.

Morales said, 'Did you go to Las Rocas?'

'Yes, but Joanna wasn't at her hotel.'

'Funny! I thought she was staying in today.'

'Got bored, maybe. Why don't you drop by on your way home?'

'I'll do that.'

'See you later.'

'Have a nice swim. Before midday.' Morales replaced the receiver, went back to the bar, and drank his orange juice reflectively.

One of the rocks sloped directly into the water; it was slippery with algae and thus only usable when the tide was high and the waves low; a boisterous sea could pull your legs away from under you, which was painful as well as dangerous; then, the only way of getting in was to make a shallow dive from higher up, and the only way of getting out was to wait for the correct surge to lift you back again:

highly satisfying when the manœuvre worked correctly, highly awkward when it didn't.

On this day following his father's death, the sea was calm, and the only moment of true terror that David experienced was when the first rush of cold water pulled at his ankles; as soon as he had skidded down the slippery rock and flung himself forward, the terror ebbed, and he knew, as he had not known a minute before, that he would be able to swim with confidence in the future.

There were further qualms naturally, the sharpest being at the moment when the current, westerly off Punto del Barranco, took him in its gentle grip and hauled him out to sea. But what you did with this current, as his father had shown him, was to allow it to have its way until it was deflected by a jagged outcrop, much frequented by a solitary scuba-diver and three seabirds; here the current lost interest in you, and half a dozen strong crawls towards the shore cast it off altogether, leaving you with a lazy swim back to the sloping rocks which were home.

Another qualm seized David at the thought of his father's body, perhaps directly beneath him, but he knew that the idea was absurd, the current would have carried it away within seconds. According to the scuba-diver, a taciturn and all but incomprehensible Swede, it operated at every depth down to the sea-bed which was dull as a consequence, scoured eternally by that fierce flow. The thought of his father made him glance out of habit towards the rocks where, if they were not swimming together, Alex Hunter would sit watching him: perhaps because he didn't trust Punto del Barranco as implicitly as he pretended he did. And there . . . !

A wave smacked David's head and filled his gaping mouth with water; he choked and resurfaced, staring. For a moment it had seemed . . . But now he realized that the figure sitting not far from his piled clothing bore no resemblance to his father at all. As he drew nearer he saw that it was a young man, fair-haired, wearing gold-rimmed glasses.

He reached the algae-covered slope and allowed a wave to lift him and propel him forward to a point at which the rock was no longer slippery; he found his footing with ease, satisfied that if there had to be a watcher he had at least contrived a neat landing, unlike many floundering, gasping attempts in the past. The young man looked British, or possibly American, though few Americans came to Tenerife and then only to Puerto with its British pubs and British smell of over-used frying oil, God alone knew what they thought of *that*! He said, 'Hi!'

Acton said, 'Hi! You're a good swimmer.'

'It's not as tricky as it looks.'

'Too tricky for me, mate. Want a beer?'

David accepted the beer, partly because he was friendly by nature, partly because he was afraid that his face might have betrayed ill-mannered resentment at this invasion of what had always been his, and his father's, privacy. (Anne didn't enjoy their kind of swimming; she and her mother either used the villa's pool or drove to a small and crowded playa some five miles away.) The young man said, 'Okay, I realize this is, you know, your private place. No good pretending I'm not here on purpose, I'm a bloody nosey-parker. Want me to push off?'

David stared, chained to the spot by the hospitable can of beer which he was already drinking. 'Nosey-parker?'

'Press,' said Acton, showing a badge pinned to the underside of his shirt-collar. 'Andrew Castle, freelance. I'm spending a few days in Puerto with the wife. Hell-hole! I read about your father in the local rag, thought there might be a story in it for me.'

They examined each other in the brilliant sunlight. Acton added, 'Well, I'm honest anyway. Want me to disappear?'

David shook his head. 'But I don't want to talk about it.'

'Okay. We know where we stand, right?'

David spread out his towel and lay on it face downwards; the sun immediately began to sear his salty back. Acton said, 'I'll hand it to you—took a bit of guts to go back in, right here, with *that* current.'

'The current's not so bad, not on a decent day.'

'Was yesterday a decent day?'

David looked up at him, squinting in the glare. Acton grimaced, playing up the honest charm which he had perfected. 'No,' said David, 'yesterday was calm too.'

'Then why do you suppose . . . ?'

At this moment there was a chatter of falling pebbles, a tall figure loomed against the sky at the top of the shaly cliff, and Patrick MacAlistair, all six feet two inches of him, came slithering down to join them.

David, surprised, jumped up and ran forward. MacAlistair hugged him with uninhibited American emotion. 'Davey, I'm so sorry, you know that—what the hell is there to say?' But his eyes were on the stranger.

Released from the hug, David said, 'This is . . . Well, he's a journalist.'

'Name of Andrew Castle.' Acton extended a hand. Patrick MacAlistair did not take it. David, who had been prepared for Patrick to be as different, following his father's death, as everybody else was, recognized with a sense of shock that he could be formidable; not just physically: with his height, his all-American good-looks, his whiteish fair hair, brilliant under this sun, he had always been that: but inwardly. He said, 'Press, huh?'

Acton shuffled his feet a little; whether it was a genuine reaction to MacAlistair's physical presence or a detail of his performance as Andrew Castle even he might have been unable to say. David felt sorry for him and also felt that his own attitude needed defining: 'Mr Castle's on holiday at Puerto; he read about it in the local paper, he was . . .' His voice trailed away because of the intensity of the stare between the other two. Patrick MacAlistair said, 'Puerto, eh? What hotel?'

'La Speranza. My wife and I . . .'

'When did you get there?'

'Saturday. We don't like it much, we thought . . .'

'Press-card?'

The shirt-collar was lifted again. MacAlistair nodded. The stare continued. David gaped. The sun crashed down, as if intending to hammer all three of them into the rock. After what seemed a long time, MacAlistair nodded again, decisively, making up his mind about something. 'Well, Mr Andrew Castle, journalist, of the Hotel La Speranza, Puerto de la Cruz, I think you should get in your car, wherever that may be, and piss off. Good idea?'

The younger man thought for a moment; then shrugged. 'Seemed worth trying.'

'We all make mistakes.'

David noticed that something in this seemingly ordinary remark angered Mr Castle, making his facial muscles contract, making him turn away abruptly. However, he took his time about climbing the cliff-path, and raised a hand in salute before disappearing. MacAlistair looked at David—who found himself transfixed by the blue-grey eyes he had known so well all his life. Had they always possessed this steely regard, or was it something to do with the light, with a reflection from the steely waves? 'Your mother thinks you came down here to . . . to brood, she'd have a fit if she knew you'd been swimming.'

David gestured, looking very young. 'I had to.'

'Sure, you had to.' He turned those eyes on the glittering ocean; then glanced at the sun, said, 'Jesus!' and withdrew to a slit of shade under the cliff. David followed. 'I thought you were getting to the airport at eleven-thirty.'

'No. I said I'd be *here* around eleven-thirty. Glad I was. What did you tell him?'

'Nothing.'

MacAlistair pondered this. 'Your mother says there was some insurance guy earlier this morning.'

'Yes.'

'Pretty darn quick off the mark! Specially for a Spaniard!'

'He was afraid we might pack up and go before he'd seen us. He said he might come back and talk to you.'

'Did he?' And after another moment's thought: 'I guess that makes sense—kind of.' When he looked up again, both the eyes and the voice had softened: 'What the hell are we going to do without your father, eh?' He shook the handsome head, struck, it seemed to David, by an unexpectedly profound sadness. How close had they been, this man and his father? He didn't know; he didn't know anything really, except that they had met years ago when they were both in their respective armies—in Frankfurt, wasn't it? He said, 'Annie thought . . . She said Father got a phone call only an hour before he died, she thought it was you, was it?'

'Said? Who to?'

'The insurance man.'

'Why was he interested?'

'There's this idea that it was suicide.'

'And Anne goes along with it.'

'Yes.'

'No, I didn't call him.' He pushed away from the cliff on which he was leaning, moved out into the sun again, stood looking down at the waves. 'Hit you pretty hard, eh Davey?'

'Yes, but . . . not how I expected. It's all . . . I can't explain. Nothing seems to be quite what I thought it was.'

Patrick MacAlistair turned and gave him another of those piercing looks, never noticed before even if they had ever existed before. 'That's it,' he said. 'Nothing ever *is* quite what you think, that's the real Catch 22.'

8

Acton drove his rented car, yet another Seat, through the bougainvillea-draped gate of La Casa Real at Playa de las Americas, and parked it neatly in spite of his anger. He went straight to Number 12, the cabin occupied by Morales, even though they had agreed not to have any public contact with each other.

His colleague was propped against the bedhead, deep in thought, dark eyebrows drawn together. Faced with Acton's anger he remained cool—which annoyed Acton all the more, Spaniards were not supposed to be cool—and said, 'The Hunter boy told me eleven-thirty at the airport, that's all I know. He must have got it wrong.'

'So *I* got it wrong!'

'It doesn't matter.'

'MacAlistair *saw* me, he's as bright as a bloody ferret, he was on to me right away.'

'Then we make sure he doesn't see you again. For God's sake, Colin! He'll probably check Señor Serrano too—so both identities are blown. So what? They were expendable.'

Acton knew that this was true; but he also knew, from a long experience of crooked dealing, though he was only twenty-seven, that the fewer people who were able to recognize you, the better.

Morales continued: 'MacAlistair didn't see *me*, and of the family only the boy saw you . . .'

'We've lost personal contact.'

'With the Hunters? Why?'

'You just said it yourself—MacAlistair will check, the identities are blown. We should have moved more slowly.'

Morales sighed. 'We moved quickly in order to get in and out before MacAlistair arrived. And it worked.'

'As far as you're concerned.'

'We're a team, Colin, there's no you or me. And even if MacAlistair finds out every damn thing about us, what makes you think he'll tell anyone else? He's got as much to hide as we have—more.'

Acton accepted this ungraciously, he hadn't thought of it.

'So you're still clean with the Hunters as long as he's not around, and I'm clean with him as long as they're not around. And we've already got the answer to two of those questions: Hunter *did* receive a telephone call just before he died, and it was probably from MacAlistair.'

'We don't know about that, not for sure.' Acton was in one of his most negative moods. 'We don't know about a lot of things, until the body shows up. If it ever does.'

'There's no sign of it yet.'

'How do you know—bar-talk?' With a slight sneer.

'Fisherman talk.' Morales was immune to Acton's sneers, and to his temper, and to his fits of negation. 'The police have asked all fishermen to co-operate.'

'Did you find Joanna?'

'Yes. Nothing wrong there. We arranged a regular routine check, morning and evening, eight o'clock.'

Acton was gazing out of the window. Beyond the little patio belonging to Number 12, beyond La Casa Real's cleverly contrived personal paradise of palms and creepers, reared the hideous pink tower of an apartment-block; beyond that the gaunt skeletons of two more, unfinished. It was said that German capital had suddenly been withdrawn, leaving these mastodons stranded in a waste of parched mud and stunted cacti. There they might well remain until they rusted into decay. What a clanging and crashing of old iron bones!

Acton said, 'Godawful place! Why does anyone come here'?

'Sun, why else?'

Acton sat down on the edge of the bed, ran his hands through his wiry hair; then took off his glasses, revealing the true, storm-trooper cast of his features. 'I don't like being checked out by MacAlistair.'

Morales didn't bother to answer. He knew that Acton had a passion for anonymity, almost, or even quite, psychotic. Acton had once told him, after a few drinks, that as a child he would hide instinctively whenever an adult approached.

9

MacAlistair was indeed checking them out: first of all the Hotel La Speranza at Puerto de la Cruz.

'Yes, señor, we have a Mr and Mrs Andrew Castle staying here. They are perhaps your friends.'

'Could be. When did they arrive?'

'Saturday, señor.' Acton had not, had never, acted blind.

'I wonder if they're in right now.'

'I'm not sure. By the pool perhaps. Shall I page them?'

'Page Mr Castle, please.'

He waited; heard the metallic voice from the hotel public address system: 'Mr Castle, Mr Andrew Castle — telephone, please.'

Presently an adenoidal British voice, outer London, said, 'Castle here, who's that?'

'My name's Travers, and I guess I've made a mistake; got the wrong Castle.'

'Sounds like it. We don't know anyone here—no Americans anyway.'

'My friend is English, in his twenties, fair hair; he's a newspaper reporter.'

'I'm English, in my fifties, no hair, sanitary engineer.'

'Mr Castle, I'm sorry to have troubled you.'

The call to West London Amalgamated's agents in Santa Cruz was just as decisive: they certainly employed a claims investigator called Serrano, but he was in Spain attending a sick father.

MacAlistair continued to sit on Catherine Hunter's bed—he was using her phone for privacy—considering what he had discovered. There was something ill-prepared and sketchy about it which surprised him: possible result of being pushed for time. He remembered that down there on those sun-blasted rocks, young David had said, 'I thought you were getting to the airport at eleven-thirty.' It didn't take much deduction to guess that he had given this information to 'Señor Serrano', and only a little more to conclude that 'Señor Serrano' must have passed it on to 'Andrew Castle'.

MacAlistair grimaced. Somewhere in the future he could discern the rough shape of an eventuality which might force him to take Alex's son into his confidence; this was a chasm he would cross, by whatever means, when he reached it. He disliked taking people into his confidence, and the dislike was not altogether selfish, it contained a degree of charity, because he knew that by the very act of confiding in anybody he automatically put that body in danger. He had no wish to put David in danger, but on the other hand he wouldn't hesitate to do so if the situation demanded it. The situation didn't demand it as yet.

During his telephone calls he had been staring at a photograph of Alex Hunter which always stood on his wife's dressing-table; now he stood up, crossed the room,

picked it up, and examined it: a lucky snapshot taken by
David during his brief attack of camera enthusiasm.
MacAlistair tried to see the face clearly, as a stranger
might see it; this wasn't easy, he knew it too well in too
many different aspects. It was a pleasant face, good-
looking, or at least attractive; the firm mouth had been
caught in a wry, lop-sided smile; a lock of brown hair fell
across the forehead, boyishly; he had been reading, the
book lay against his chest, and the glasses were poised in
one hand, ready to be replaced. But it was the eyes which
fascinated MacAlistair, as they always had, because
however much Alex Hunter might change, and he could
change a great deal, the eyes remained the same. Sharp,
intense, unaffected by the smile which softened the
mouth, they were oddly inhuman, fixed on something
further away than the family garden in which the camera
had caught him: fixed on heroic dreams, illusions, vistas
of eternity: the eyes of a saint or of a madman.

MacAlistair heard footsteps approaching. Most men
would have put the photograph down immediately, but
he had imposed other disciplines upon himself, and
allowed Catherine Hunter to find him holding it. She
said, 'The policeman's here.'

MacAlistair replaced the photograph. They both
stared at it. She added, 'Everything all right in London?'
His excuse had been business.

'Yes, fine.'

'It was nice of you to drop everything and come here.'

'For God's sake, what else would I have done?'

They were still looking at the likeness, if that's what it
was, of Alex Hunter. Frowning, she said, 'We mustn't let
that . . . foolishness affect us now, Patrick — our attitude
towards each other.'

'I can't see why it should; it never has.'

'It was my fault, I was probably drunk.'

'Both our faults. And bad luck for both of us that we

both loved him.'

Two years before, during one of her husband's
interminable absences, he had taken her out to dinner. A
rare, warm London evening when the shabby city seemed
to retrieve a few scraps of its old, long-lost charm. The
food had been good, the wine copious. He had walked her
home across the park, and at some point, crossing a street
perhaps, had taken her hand; not relinquished it.

After the first few seconds this began to seem quite
normal. Asking him in for a nightcap was normal too,
practically a habit, the difference being that on this
occasion Alex wasn't there. They sat on the sofa in her
drawing-room, windows wide open, listening to the sound
of a party on the far side of the square. She knew that he
was going to kiss her and was looking forward to it. He did
so; it was mutually agreeable; one thing then led swiftly to
another. Two good-looking people, old friends, he no
longer married, her husband absent, children at
school . . .

And then, as if he were in the room with them and not
many thousands of miles away in Hong Kong, Alex
slipped between them. Both were in a state of sexual
excitement, and both knew that they would never go
through with it. Extrication, physical and social, was
bound to be awkward; fortunately emotion had never
been involved. On the whole, they prided themselves to
themselves afterwards, they hadn't done too badly.
Catherine retired to the kitchen to make coffee and
regain her composure, leaving MacAlistair alone in the
drawing-room. On her return they hadn't discussed the
incident very much, there was no need, and they had
never referred to it thereafter. Until now. It was as if Alex
Hunter's death, and his photograph, demanded some
reference to it. Catherine said, 'I never told him, of
course.'

'What was there to tell?' He felt her shy away from this,

and, adept at sensing what people imagined was hidden, wondered whether there were other secrets. If so, Alex had deserved it.

'If I *had* told him, would he have said anything to you?'

'Probably not.'

She nodded, eyeing him. 'And anyway you wouldn't admit it, not even now that he's dead.'

Her acceptance of this triangular duplicity disturbed him: on one level. 'What makes you think so?'

'There's nothing I don't know about loyalty. But it's all hypothetical.'

'Yes.'

She looked at the photograph again. 'Did he . . . keep things from me?'

'I wouldn't know.'

'You would, you do. All that time he was abroad. Half our lifetime together, I sometimes used to think.' She sighed deeply, and turned away. To the distant ocean she said, 'I miss him, Patrick, painfully. I didn't think I would, I didn't think I cared.

'Of course you cared.'

'Absence makes the heart grow fonder?' She gave him a quizzical look over her shoulder. 'Does it or doesn't it? Please go and talk to that policeman, poor Davey will be having an awful time.'

Thus dismissed by the General's daughter, MacAlistair went out of the room and down the stairs. He was glad she didn't know the real reason for his drawing back on that warm summer night two years ago: less to do with Alex than with the fact that he liked her. The truth was that behind Patrick MacAlistair's blue-grey eyes lay an arctic waste in which liking (he didn't know much about love, and had certainly not loved his mother and father) was forever separated from lust; he had never liked any of the women he had lusted after, neither had he ever lusted after anyone he liked. Somewhere within this schizoid

state of affairs, he supposed, lay the clue to his relationship with Alex Hunter: the closest relationship he had
ever known or ever would know.

From the living-room came the sound of a crippled
conversation in Spanish. MacAlistair went towards it.
David's relief at the sight of him was visibly apparent;
Lieutenant Dominguez bowed politely. It took the two
men all of five minutes to recognize that by some chance
they were brothers under the skin: a recognition which
was to have ironical, and eventually disastrous, consequences.

When MacAlistair gestured towards the terrace,
indicating that their conversation should take place
outside rather than in the house, Dominguez complied
without demur; it would be much too hot on the terrace,
but the tall American doubtless had an excellent reason
for choosing to talk there.

David's understanding of the exchange which now took
place was fragmented: by linguistic exhaustion, by his
having had a second glass of wine with his lunch, on top
of beer, and by the fact that MacAlistair's Spanish,
though swift and fluent, had been learned in Mexico and
was inclined to ignore the purities of Iberian pronun-
ciation. However, Lieutenant Dominguez evidently found
it easy to understand him; twins can often communicate
without the use of words anyway.

Very properly, MacAlistair asked for an account of
police thinking as regards the death of his friend and
partner. Dominguez supplied it concisely. There seemed
to be no reason to suspect suicide, and there was no
evidence to suggest it; murder for motives unknown must
naturally remain a possibility until the body was found
and forensic examination dismissed it; therefore at the
moment, and in spite of Señor Hunter's known prowess as
a swimmer, accident seemed the most likely explanation—unless of course Señor MacAlistair was about to

produce new evidence to the contrary. Señor MacAlistair, who had been sizing the policeman up during all this, could produce no new evidence; moreover, he agreed one hundred per cent with the Lieutenant's hypothesis.

So much David understood, largely because he had heard most of it before; and it was at this point that MacAlistair suggested that their guest might care for some refreshment. Dominguez, who never drank during the day or when he was on duty, said that he would very much like a brandy with ice and a great deal of soda. David went to get it.

MacAlistair and the policeman then turned to the low wall edging the terrace; side by side they gazed down at the glittering ocean which now, with the sun at its full height, seemed to be hammered out of millions of steel sequins; it looked as if it would not so much drown a man as scrape him to death.

MacAlistair said, 'The fact that the body has not yet been found must be a great inconvenience to your enquiries.'

'Worse, señor, it makes my life unbearable.'

'How so?'

'We depend upon our tourist industry. All our tourists know of this death; they are asking why it has not been explained, not . . . tidied up. I speak frankly.'

MacAlistair said nothing, knowing that there was more to come and, coming from a man like Dominguez, that there was probably something behind it.

'My superior, an unpleasant man, is being harassed by *his* superior, and therefore gives me no peace. I cannot conjure up dead bodies to oblige him.'

'Hardly.'

The Lieutenant flashed a swift glance, no more. 'I pray,' he said to the Atlantic, 'that this body will be discovered soon — identification will already be distressing for the señora. As for myself, if I may mention the matter in the same breath, I am shortly expecting promotion.'

MacAlistair considered all this, and then said, 'Tell me, Lieutenant, is it necessary by law for the señora to undergo the ordeal of identification?'

'No. We demand only that the person has known the victim intimately for a reasonable period of time.'

The afternoon heat was heavy, the sea's glitter well-nigh unbearable; yet both ordeals seemed to suit the gist of the conversation. From the villa came the sound of David talking to his mother; MacAlistair welcomed it as a sign that refreshment would be delayed. He said with care, 'Lieutenant Dominguez, are you in a position to intercept and record long-distance telephone calls from this part of the island?'

'There are few exchanges, señor, compared with the North.'

'Then calls from the area under your authority could be intercepted?'

'*All* calls?'

'No. Only those to London.'

Dominguez did not assent, and MacAlistair didn't expect him to; more needed to be said. 'As regards identification, I see no reason to distress the señora or her children. I myself am prepared to identify the body, if that suits you.'

Now they both turned from the ocean and examined each other closely. At length Dominguez said, 'The number of long-distance calls from this area to London is limited, most of the British go to Puerto, as you know. I think I could help you, providing the reason seemed to me . . . logical.'

No scruple prevented MacAlistair from taking a man like Dominguez into his confidence—to an extent. Danger was the Spaniard's business, indeed he was himself dangerous; this was only one of the things they had instantly known about each other. He said, 'The reason is that strangers have been to this house enquiring into Señor Hunter's death.'

The Lieutenant nodded, dark eyes fixed on Mac-Alistair's face; he knew that he wasn't being told the entire truth, only a fool would have expected that, but the measure of the untruth was just as important.

'Naturally,' continued MacAlistair, 'a woman like the señora, a widow, well-to-do, is at the mercy of certain kinds of people; it's my duty to protect her.'

'Who are these . . . strangers?'

'I don't know, but I think they come from England, and are acting under instructions from England. Interception of a single lucky telephone conversation might well give us the answer.'

The policeman said nothing, because the ball was still in MacAlistair's court. 'Since we have a common interest in this matter of identification—you, your superior, and myself—I feel it presents only a minor problem. Of administration perhaps. Am I correct?'

A tinkling sound from the direction of the villa signalled the return of David with the cooling drink which the guest didn't want anyway. As he came into view, carrying a tall glass, Dominguez said quietly, 'You are correct, señor, so long as I have your word that you alone will undertake the task of identification.'

'You have my word.'

The Lieutenant turned to David, took the drink, thanked him courteously, and sipped as little of it as possible. Looking back at the tall, fair American with whom he had established such instant and satisfactory accord, he added, 'I am most pleased to have had this talk with you, señor.'

'And I can take it that we're agreed on essentials?'

'Indeed yes, I shall keep you closely informed. The afternoon is very hot, don't you think?'

MacAlistair gestured towards the shade of the house, at

the same time putting a hand on David's shoulder and propelling him towards it. As soon as the young man's back was turned, the Lieutenant emptied three-quarters of the contents of his glass over the edge of the terrace, sending the lizards scuttling. In doing so, he caught MacAlistair's eye. Both of them smiled.

Both of them were unaware of the fact that David, ahead of them, had witnessed the whole intimate charade reflected in the picture window of the living-room. Admittedly they themselves were so placed that they couldn't see the reflection, but under other circumstances experience would have warned them instantly that such a reflection might well exist. Perhaps that mutual recognition, not to mention the speed and precision with which they'd both made use of it, had hypnotized them with a sense of their own cleverness. The darkness of the interior, the stark sunlight on the terrace, made the window into a giant mirror; and in this mirror David Hunter had seen exactly how much his life had changed, how much his manner of *seeing* it had changed, since his father's death. David Through The Looking-Glass! MacAlistair's brief conspiratorial smile, the knowledge that in some way the two men were playing a game with him, made him realize that perhaps he had never in all these years truly trusted his father's friend and partner. Why otherwise had he put that surprising question to his mother last night, 'Do you like him?' And, yes — why had Annie, in answer to tidings of MacAlistair's approach, said, 'And fuck him too!'

The reflected incident had not merely nudged the chess-board but sent it crashing to the floor, the pieces scattered, some of them for all he knew broken beyond repair.

Anne, found once again in her bedroom, but this time prettifying herself for reasons which her brother could not comprehend, said, 'I just don't like him, that's all, I never have.'

'Why didn't you say so?'

'I was never asked. And anyway, what's the point? I mean, there he *is*! It's like saying you don't like the grandfather clock on the stairs at home.'

'Don't you?'

'I detest it.' She fiddled with her hair, no longer lank but lustrous from washing and brushing. Mysterious girl.

'How can you detest a clock?'

'That awful hollow tock-tack and the way it strikes, like a funeral bell.' She had said it without thinking of her father, and so caught her breath, face crumpling. David waited for tears, but she made a visible effort and restrained them, looking at that moment like a plainer version of her mother.

David persisted: 'Why don't you like Patrick?'

She glanced at his reflection in the mirror, and was struck by his earnest expression; she thought carefully for a while and then said, 'Well, I think he's a phoney.'

'In what way?'

'Gosh, aren't you nosey all of a sudden?'

'No, Annie — why phoney?'

'Intuition,' said his sister with finality; she might be fifteen and young for her age but she knew the value of this magical word when it came to silencing the male. But for good measure she added, 'Also he had the hots for Ma.'

It always astonished David that she could veer so abruptly from holier-than-thou to hoyden. 'Oh, come on, Annie, that's bollocks!'

She shrugged.

'How do you know? And if you say "intuition" again I'll slug you.'

'I don't *know*, it's a feeling I had — ages ago. Anyway what does it matter? at least he's getting us all out of this creepy house for a bit.'

It seemed that Patrick MacAlistair had suggested a

drive up to the cooler slopes of Tiede, a walk in the pine
forests. It was true that the afternoon was stifling; the
wind had dropped and a veil of mist obscured the top of
the extinct volcano, which meant that on the other, lush,
side of the island the packaged British were lying in neat
rows beside their hotel swimming-pools under thick
cloud. Here on the southern, desert slopes, so different
that they might have been on another continent, the sun
would continue to blaze, burning up the windless day
until it exploded in thunder towards evening; and even
then, the rain would not fall here but in that other world
on the far side of El Tiede.

10

Colin Acton sat with his back against a banana palm, lost
in the deep green shadow at the edge of the plantation. A
pair of powerful binoculars stood on a tripod straddling
his legs; through them he watched Mrs Hunter and her
daughter climb into the car which MacAlistair had
rented at the airport: no beat-up Seat for him, a
Mercedes. David Hunter did not get in with them,
apparently he was staying behind. Mrs Hunter rolled
down a window, speaking to him.

She was saying, 'David, you won't swim in the sea, will
you? There's always the pool.'

David hated the pool, it was too warm and the water
had a syrupy texture; but he was noticing how, daily even
hourly, his mother seemed to be growing more frail, more
tense. On the evening of his father's death she had said, 'I
feel numb'; now it looked as though the numbness was
wearing off like an anaesthetic leaving only the pain; and
so he promised not to put so much as a toe in the Atlantic.

Anne, in the back seat, was wearing a pi, keep-out

expression to go with her burnished hair and mysteriously
renovated face; she wasn't even pretending to be sorry
that her brother had declined to accompany them. As for
MacAlistair—since the incident witnessed through the
Looking-Glass, David had embarked upon another
laborious process of reassessment; obviously there was
more to the man than met the eye, and yet what did meet
the eye was so seeming-true, so polished, that again and
again he lost his nerve and began to doubt his own
doubts. As the car moved away he found himself wishing
that he had gone with them; and then rejected the wish as
childish.

Acton, from his carefully sited position on the hillside,
could follow the Mercedes all the way to the main road,
with only minor visual interruptions; he swivelled the
heavy binoculars, refocusing, and caught up with the car
just as it took a left fork, mounting towards the foothills of
Tiede. He made a note of the time and turned the
binoculars back to the villa. David Hunter was still
standing on the driveway, kicking aimlessly at gravel.

Out in the harsh sunlight cicadas kept up their tireless
whirr and hiss; in the shadows a myriad flies amused
themselves by trying to drive Acton mad. He thought
bitterly of Morales, sitting with a cool drink in the café
opposite the police station in Las Rocas. Dominguez had
commandeered an office there for use as a temporary
headquarters. Morales was waiting to see what he would
do next. Being a Spaniard he would certainly take a
siesta, thus ensuring a nice easy afternoon for Morales.
Whereas Acton himself was stuck out here on this God-
forsaken, fly-infested hillside . . .

He wiped the sweat from his face and took another look
at David Hunter; he was now staring out over the ocean,
face screwed up against the glare. After a moment he
seemed to make up his mind about something; moved
across the drive and down a flight of steps, obviously

heading for the rocks, but not by the path which Acton had seen him use before; this was a longer route following a dry crumbling wall which encircled a field of tomatoes; it dropped more swiftly away from the villa and, Acton guessed, was probably invisible from its windows. The boy appeared to be looking for something. Yes, definitely: searching the ground with careful attention.

Acton sat back against the banana palm, thinking. Morales had stressed the importance of maintaining a continuous watch on the villa, but the villa was now empty, and anyway who was Morales to stress importances? To Acton it was of vital importance that he had been seen by MacAlistair, if not for who he was then certainly for what he was; the child had hidden from strangers instinctively, the man could not resist the urge to know whether MacAlistair had checked out 'Andrew Castle' and, more importantly, whether he had shared his findings with the Hunter family. If he had *not* shared them . . . Well, that left interesting possibilities, and any one of these might prove a great deal more valuable than watching an empty villa.

In this Acton was prescient, but then he often was; and why not? Hadn't he started his career of lies and evasion at a singularly early age, becoming a junior pastmaster by the time he was eight?

He got to his feet, gathered up the heavy binoculars and the tripod, and went swiftly through the green gloom of the plantation, slashed by blades of sunlight, to the place where he had hidden his car.

David continued a slow progress towards the rocks, searching for some sign of his father's reading glasses, thinking about MacAlistair, occasionally pausing to wonder whether there were not ways of improving the local methods of tomato cultivation — the yield per acre could only be . . . No, no! MacAlistair was more important; that reflected glimpse of him in secret communion with Lieutenant Dominguez had opened up a whole vista of Looking-Glass images stretching away into the past. Once, when he was said to be doing business in Portugal, David had definitely seen him in Oxford Street; once, when David had written to his father in Houston, the reply had come from MacAlistair, who wasn't even supposed to *be* in Houston, saying that Alex Hunter had been called unexpectedly to Chicago and wanted him, MacAlistair, to answer the boy's letter; once, when MacAlistair had come to dinner and departed quite early, at about ten-thirty, adolescent David, unable to sleep, mooning at his bedroom window, had watched him actually leaving at two o'clock in the morning.

There was nothing conclusively sinister about any of these instances, or in a dozen more which sprang to mind as soon as he supplied them with a springboard, but they were peculiar, suspicious. And anyway, how the hell did a man like MacAlistair come to *have* secret communion with a man like Dominguez after only ten minutes' conversation? And how strange that both his mother ('he's always been there, hasn't he?') and his sister ('I mean, there he *is*!') had both adopted the same attitude towards MacAlistair's omnipotence. David himself had probably shared it, but not any more. Oh no, not any more! And then there was Annie's contention that MacAlistair had at one time 'had the hots' for their mother? If this was true — and he was no longer so dismissive of her opinions — what had been the outcome? A beautiful woman whose husband was always away . . .

It took him several seconds, thus preoccupied with his thoughts, to realize that he was staring at the smashed remnants of his father's glasses: or rather at a thousand glittering particles of glass lying on the baked earth between two stones. Of course the hillside was littered with broken bottles, the tomato-pickers left a yearly drift of them, but in this case . . . He knelt swiftly, rolled one of the stones aside and revealed the squashed frame of the glasses.

This was strange, almost as strange as Patrick MacAlistair. His father never used this path; why had he used it when going down for what would be his final swim? And the glasses had not merely been dropped, they had been deliberately destroyed; somebody had ground the lenses on to the stone and then hidden the frame under it. Why? Did this constitute evidence: of an attempt to mislead investigation, of a struggle, even of murder? If it did, why wasn't David Hunter, the dead man's son, taking it directly to the police? Of course the answer lay in a certain look which the police had exchanged with the dead man's friend and partner at the moment of emptying an unwanted drink over the edge of a terrace.

David was about to stand up—the sun was clubbing the back of his neck—when he saw, lying in the shadow of the second stone, an intact piece of lens about the size of his thumb-nail; and he had just collected this, slipping it into his shirt pocket with the battered frame, when he heard the sound of a car. He straightened up. At the same moment the car came to a standstill some thirty yards away where the road, no more than a dusty track used for the transport of tomatoes and bananas, crossed the path. He recognized the driver at once: Andrew Castle, the pleasant journalist to whom MacAlistair had been so curtly rude. Acton raised a hand in greeting. David moved towards him.

High up on Mount Tiede's southern foothills, but below the extraordinary volcanic plateau with its moon landscape and proliferating craters, Catherine Hunter, Patrick MacAlistair, and Anne walked in single file, and in that order, under the pines. The air was cool and fragrant, and the veil of cloud across the peak cast a pleasant moist shade broken every now and again by shafts of pale sunlight, very unlike the sledgehammer sun of the coast.

Single file was necessary because the path skirted a deep ravine; it was also a formation which suited all three of them who, for different reasons, preferred their own thoughts to idle conversation.

Catherine Hunter was free to consider all over again the paradox of her husband's death, of which she was becoming more and more aware; hence the intensifying frailty and tension noted by her son. Alive, Alex had enraged her with his awful absences and his cat-like, tomcat-like, attitude towards them: to the point where she had more than once wished him dead. Yes, at all costs she would be honest. But upon his returning she had hated herself for her own suspicion and distrust, because he was so obviously a kind and good man who loved her in his own strange way.

Dead, he presented her with a far more complex and surprising problem, in that now, too late, she was beginning to realize how much *she* had loved *him*; depended upon him too. But this time he would never return; this was the final absence.

Anne Hunter, bringing up the rear of the column, had not exactly forgotten her father's death, a chance word could revive the tears at any time; but something else had moved to the forefront of her mind, causing her to exchange the role of Nun for that of Electra: they had been doing the play at school. Ahead of her walked Clytemnestra, the sinful mother, and the lustful paramour Aegisthus; her brother, Orestes, as yet unmindful of his part, needless to say, was loitering elsewhere, leaving Electra to bear her knowledge and humiliation alone — what heroism! — until he should come to his senses and join her in avenging the death of their noble father.

Unfortunately there were flaws in this reconstruction, for Electra had never, as far as Anne knew, fancied Aegisthus, whereas she herself . . . Well, it had to be admitted that Patrick MacAlistair was a very attractive man. It was true that she didn't *like* him, but apparently that had little to do with the other thing, and she found it quite impossible to keep her eyes away from the back of his head, the way his hair lay, what would it be like to touch, soft or wiry? No, perhaps she wasn't Electra after all, and as for him, he hadn't even noticed the trouble she had taken with her appearance.

This was true. MacAlistair was unaware of either female, totally engrossed in practicalities; mapping out the possible course of the evening, the morrow, the day after. Circumstance prevented him from planning ahead, but at all costs he must think ahead and thus reduce the danger of some unconsidered detail leaping out of the darkness to stab him in the back. His agreement with Lieutenant Dominguez, and the lurking presence of 'Andrew Castle' and 'Señor Serrano', and conceivably of others unknown, introduced permutations which must be anticipated from every point of view. And so, as solitary as if he were on his own, he was following a dozen different paths apart from the one he trod beneath the pines: supposing Dominguez failed to honour his side of their contract . . . ? supposing 'Castle' and 'Serrano' had been sent to Tenerife to watch his own movements . . . ? supposing there existed, somewhere, actual proof that he himself had indeed telephoned Alex Hunter less than an hour before his death . . . ?

It had taken Acton only a few minutes, perhaps even seconds, to reassure himself that MacAlistair had not said a word about his false identity, not to David Hunter anyway. Almost as quickly he had become aware of something else, a nuance, the exact nature of which eluded him: as yet — he was in full pursuit of it.

They were now walking in silence along the rocks. A storm far out in the Atlantic had put the ocean in a vile temper; every now and again a huge wave would come rushing towards them, savagely intent on self-destruction: a wall of green water, a roaring, flashing surge of spray leaping high into the sun. Twice they had been compelled to jump for it, laughing, the undertow pulling hungrily at their legs. The laughter and the silence at length came to constitute a kind of camaraderie which moved David to say, 'I'm sorry about yesterday; he's . . . an old friend of the family, I suppose he thinks he has to . . . protect us.'

'He could be right.'

'Yes, but . . .' Acton was quick to sense unspoken criticism; the evasive factor became a little clearer. 'Seemed okay to me. Good-looking bastard!'

David remained silent. Acton felt it safe to go a step further: 'Don't you like him then?'

'He's all right.'

Acton now saw it clearly: David Hunter *didn't* like MacAlistair. That was interesting, even promising. He inserted a small lever, nothing clumsy, the boy wasn't stupid. 'I wouldn't have thought there was any need for him to come rushing out here. You could handle the official end of it yourself, surely?'

'Yes, but you know how they are.'

'God, yes! Sometimes I used to think they didn't *want* me to grow up.'

'Mother's pretty good about it.'

'Mine wasn't.' He couldn't even remember his mother, she had decamped with another man when he was three years old. 'I suppose you'll be going home soon.'

'We can't. Can we?'

'Sorry, I forgot! No news?'

'No. They've asked all the fishermen to keep an eye open.' He glanced out over the fierce, flashing waves. 'I don't see why they should ever find him.'

'Tough on your mother.'

'Yes. I think it's beginning to get her down. The police . . .' In his mind's eye he saw the tilting glass, the unwanted brandy and soda slopping over the wall of the terrace. 'I'm not sure I trust them.'

'*Trust* them! You're joking!' To justify his reappearance, Acton had already explained that he and 'the wife' were moving to this side of the island because Puerto was like a holiday camp and, moreover, sunless; he had also indicated that as a news story the death of Alex Hunter was generating little interest, and that he personally was not going to pursue it unless some unforeseen development occurred. Now he added to this by saying, 'Who's the copper on the case, know his name?'

'Fellow called Dominguez.'

Acton allowed a pause, as if for thought. 'Tell you what—I'll keep my ears open, we papparazzi get to hear most of the rumours. If I think the police are playing silly buggers I'll give you a tinkle.'

'Thanks. I do feel kind of . . . cut off out here.' He was touched by this thoughtful generosity. There had to be something very wrong with Patrick MacAlistair if he'd been unable to see that Castle was simply a young freelance journalist trying to earn a living. To think that yesterday, at this very spot, he had found MacAlistair formidable! He wasn't formidable at all, he was an arrogant, lying, secretive son-of-a-bitch!

Acton saw something of this written on the youthful face, or sensed it. 'However, in view of the fact that the Press isn't exactly Number One On The Charts around here, you'd better not tell anybody we met again.'

'Don't worry, I won't.' MacAlistair wasn't the only one who could be secretive.

Again Acton allowed a thought-like pause: nothing was ever gained from hurrying a patsy. He said, 'I suppose if I do give you a ring I'd better use another name.'

'Good idea. Something I can remember.'

'Like what?'

'Henry Crannock.'

'Who the hell's he?'

'Scientist. Agricultural botany.'

So it was settled. Acton didn't for a moment believe that this contact would pay off, but it soothed the hiding child in him, the passion for anonymity; and in his experience any contact was worth making and maintaining. He didn't know what Morales would think, and he didn't much care; as far as he was concerned it had proved to be a profitable afternoon.

11

Morales was driving along the coast road heading north. There was a reasonable amount of traffic, and mercifully Lieutenant Dominguez, half a mile ahead of him, seemed to be in no hurry to get back to Santa Cruz; the police car could have outstripped the rattling Seat in a matter of seconds.

They had passed the somnolent volcano at Guimar and the basilica of Candelaria with its mysterious row of unchristian statues turning their backs upon the sea. Presently, as they approached the town, Morales would have to push his miserable little rented car to its limits and draw as close as he dared; but in the meantime he could easily keep Dominguez in sight while his mind strayed restlessly over the problems which faced him. Not the least of these was Acton. Morales was supposed to be in charge of him, but as he well knew, the only way to be 'in charge' of Acton was to treat him as an exact equal. He was probably at this very moment disobeying

Morales's 'suggestion' that the Hunters' villa should be watched at all times; yet Morales had to admit that his colleague possessed an uncanny sense of priorities, almost a sixth sense, which he himself lacked. The point was that Acton was an animal and reacted like one. No Catholic upbringing stood between him and the bald reality of the moment: no moral sense, no conscience, no scruple of any kind.

At Tabalba, Morales increased speed, and by Santa Maria del Mar there was only a single Volkswagen bus, full of grinning children, between the two cars. Since he could not afford to be separated from his quarry by traffic-lights, Morales now manoeuvred himself into position immediately behind the police car. He put on a pair of sunglasses which to some extent hid his noticeable eyebrows—he had once had them plucked but they soon returned, more luxuriant than ever—and a straw hat which made him look older, if ridiculous. But the Lieutenant seemed to be lost in his own thoughts and almost oblivious of his surroundings. There was an awkward moment when he suddenly decided to stop and park in a no-parking area, an unfair advantage indulged in by policemen the world over, but luckily a van drew out of a space some distance ahead of him, and Morales was able to slip into it, infuriating a lady driver who undoubtedly had prior claim. She was still berating him in unladylike terms when the Lieutenant walked by; Morales suffered the abuse until he was a dozen yards away; then got out of the car and went after him.

He was not sure just *why* he had decided to shadow Dominguez, following him like this into his home territory, but the policeman's behaviour on reaching the main street, the Pilar, encouraged him to believe that intuition had guided him on to the correct course. The Lieutenant sauntered slowly under the trees; then crossed the road and sauntered back; glanced at his watch, and stood staring into the window of a bookshop. The meeting when it came was so casually contrived that it seemed, even to Morales, a mere chance encounter with another member of the Guardia Civil; he almost expected Dominguez to excuse himself and move away from his colleague as soon as the person he was really waiting for appeared on the scene. But this did not happen; the two policemen, chatting amiably, walked to a café, chose a table well away from other customers; settled there for a cup of coffee.

Morales found himself stranded, with absolutely no chance of getting near enough to lip-read let alone hear what was being said, even if he risked entering the café and thus drawing attention to himself. After some thought, during which he in his turn gazed blankly into a shop window, he decided on discretion (wondering sourly if Acton would have chosen valour) and retired to another café, from which, when the traffic allowed, he could see the two men deep in conversation on the far side of the street. At one point Dominguez handed over what looked like some documents, and perhaps a photograph. His companion was of the same rank, but older, somewhat seedy; he was also sycophantic, smiling when Dominguez smiled, growing serious when Dominguez grew serious. There was no doubt that the younger man had the upper hand and wasn't afraid to show it; Morales wouldn't have been in the least surprised to learn that he possessed information which, properly placed, could cause painful embarrassment to his colleague; even from a distance it was possible to discern this kind of imbalance in their relationship.

The conjecture led Morales to a decision; when the two officers parted he would abandon Dominguez and follow the other; if the trail merely led to a nearby police station that would be too bad.

But the trail did not lead to a police station; the older

officer walked only a little way along the Pilar, turned
down a side street, and disappeared into a large building
which Morales identified with interest as a hospital.
There were a number of people milling about in the
lobby, and Morales, who could at any time have been
mistaken for an earnest young Spanish doctor, joined
them.

The policeman was talking to a porter behind an
information desk. Morales studied a notice-board at
right-angles to it, learning that visiting hours were to be
altered from the 1st of April and that the hospital football
team would be playing the army on Saturday evening
next. Meanwhile the porter had spoken on the telephone,
replaced the receiver, and was saying, loud enough for
Morales to hear, that Dr Zamora would be available in
five minutes if the officer wished to go directly to his
department. Since he added no instructions it was clear
that this was not the policeman's first visit to the
department in question. Morales followed at a distance,
a patient on a wheeled stretcher separating them, down a
long corridor smelling of disinfectant. The policeman
turned to the right and pushed open a swing door which
gave on to a descending staircase. The stretcher
continued forward; its occupant was obviously not yet
ready for Dr Zamora, whose speciality was indicated by a
sign over the door: Mortuary.

12

David Hunter was sitting on his bed staring in perplexity
at all that remained of his father's glasses. The frame
presented no particular problem except that the manner
in which it had been mangled implied violence; no, it was
the small piece of lens which was causing the deep crease

in David's forehead. He held it up to the window again;
then held it over the book which lay open on his knees; in
neither case did it distort the image. He turned it over;
the side of the glass now uppermost was slightly rounded;
this was the side at which one looked when Alex Hunter
had glanced up from his reading, brown eyes a little
owlish because of the lenses. Again David held it to the
window; mountain and sea were blurred, merging: he
looked through it at the book; the words were magnified,
not a great deal but unmistakably.

The implication was disturbing: the glasses were false,
giving the onlooker an impression of magnification and
distortion while the wearer, having no need of reading
glasses anyway, saw everything plain.

David didn't like this at all. He tried to reject the
premise: obviously he had made a mistake, it was the
inner, rounded surface which had lain next to his father's
eye, giving some slight intensification which he had
needed, and it was the flat surface which faced the world.
Unfortunately there was no escape in this direction;
David was not an unobservant young man, and, for God's
sake! how many times had he looked at the glasses on his
father's nose, been sent to fetch them, cleaned them
even? He *knew* that the rounded plane had always been
outermost, and therefore he knew, now, that his father
had not needed the glasses to read with.

But why the pretence? All right, at business meetings
perhaps, a prop, a property, something to fiddle with in
an awkward moment, to gain time with, before having to
make an important decision. But in the bosom of his own
family! Always, without exception, ever since David could
remember!

He stood up and began to pace nervously about the
bedroom. Perhaps if he tried very hard he could banish
this unhappy discovery to the incalculable and therefore
reassuring limbo of psychology; people did strange things

for little apparent reason, took refuge in unimaginably odd corners, and if his father had been that insecure . . . But his father had not, had never, been insecure; and therefore this revelation, like the revelation of MacAlistair's mysterious alliance with the Spanish policeman, opened up further Dali-esque vistas peopled by nightmare figures. If his father had falsified this seemingly unimportant detail, what other larger falsifications had he indulged in at the expense of his family? And why?

David felt, and indeed looked, if he had cared to glance in the mirror, like a child faced for the first time with the awful knowledge that grown-ups are also afraid, also weep. Childlike, he wished that he had never thought of the damned glasses in the first place, let alone allowed them to become an obsession.

Grasping at straws, he decided that the least he could do, before judging his father out of hand, was to seek an expert opinion; if he couldn't find an optician in Las Rocas who spoke fluent English—no juggling with vital technicalities in his deficient Spanish—this would have to wait until he returned to London.

A crunching of gravel outside the window heralded the return of the mountaineers. Glancing out, but keeping well behind the half-closed shutters (was secrecy catching?) David noticed that his mother looked even more brittle and uncertain than when she had set out a couple of hours before. The sudden realization that Alex Hunter had for all these years been hoodwinking her too, with his phoney glasses and with what else? momentarily caused his son to hate him. Before going down to meet them he hid the battered frame and the tell-tale piece of glass in a pile of clean shirts. The knowledge of them lay in his stomach as hard and as jagged as if he had eaten them.

13

'Five-nine-seven-nine.'

'Peter here. They've reported. Busy day by the sound of it.' From the public telephone-box, a different one every time, the prematurely white-haired young man could hear the strains of Puccini, fortissimo. The volume was reduced and the fat voice said, 'All right. Go on.'

'Morales's move paid off pretty well. Mrs Hunter and the son were cagey, but the girl came out with the whole schmeer. Hunter *did* get a phone call, an hour before he died, and it was probably from MacAlistair.'

'What do you mean, probably?' The fat man had taken a shower and was now cutting his toenails, plump left leg resting on plump right leg, bulbous stomach almost but not quite impeding his vision. He was sweating, but that was because he always kept the central-heating too high. Outside the window, dry, parsimonious snow was drifting indecisively across London; he loathed snow, it curdled his Italian blood.

He listened, grunting occasionally, to a full account of the activities of Acton and Morales, from the latter's visit to the villa as a representative of West London Amalgamated to the eight o'clock check on Joanna's welfare. When it was over he said, 'We should've bugged that house before the Hunters went there, then we'd *know* what MacAlistair said to the policeman.'

'We wouldn't. They talked out on the terrace.'

'Trust MacAlistair!' He lay back thoughtfully, pulling a vast towelling robe across his belly. He could hear the younger man's quick breathing on the other end of the line and guessed that he'd be freezing his balls off in the telephone-box. 'Mortuary, eh?'

'That's what Morales said.'

'What's going on over there?'

'I could make a few guesses.'

'You're not in the guessing business.'

The white-haired young man grimaced at the snub and continued to stamp his feet which were turning to ice. He could just see the fat slob sitting there in his overheated flat with his Puccini and his speechless blondes and God knew what else. There were times when he wouldn't have minded getting the hell out of the whole business; but that wasn't always wise, people who got out also got dead, sometimes not always, particularly if they knew as much as he did. So stamp the feet and bear it! He stamped his feet and bore it; he knew better than to interrupt the thought-processes.

Whatever they were he wasn't invited to share them. The heavy voice said, 'Get back to Morales. Tell him to report directly to me as soon as anything breaks, day or night.'

'I thought I was never to make the contact.'

'Don't think, just do it!'

14

At nine-thirty the following morning Lieutenant Dominguez telephoned the villa. Anne took the call, fetched MacAlistair from the terrace and handed him the receiver, smiling prettily. It was true that he smiled back, but so absently that even she could not convince herself that he had actually noticed her.

'Yes, Lieutenant?'

'Good morning, señor. I have interesting news for you regarding the identification we discussed yesterday.'

'Excellent.'

Dominguez knew instinctively from the other man's tone of voice that he was not alone. This was correct: apart from Anne, all ears, dawdling near the window, Catherine Hunter was drinking her morning coffee on the terrace, while David, perched on the wall, untangled a fishing-line. MacAlistair was relieved that at least none of them was out of sight, which could mean within reach of the extension phone upstairs. However, care was still called for, because though they didn't speak fluent Spanish it is one of those languages which can often be understood quite easily. Dominguez added, 'I also think that I may have some telephone conversations which will interest you.'

'You don't waste time, Lieutenant.'

'Life is short. My superior, of whom I spoke, is now resorting to veiled threats. I have not, incidentally, told him or anyone else what I'm telling you.'

'I shall respect the confidence.'

'It seems to me that you may wish to . . . make certain arrangements before meeting me in Las Rocas — I'm thinking chiefly of the son.'

'True, true.' There had been considerable indecision and argument as to how yet another day of waiting was to be passed; the only definite fact to emerge had been David's preference, yet again, for his own company. MacAlistair suspected that the boy didn't like him very much: a matter of the utmost unimportance as long as his own interests weren't in any way threatened, and David's desire for solitude didn't appear to constitute a threat, indeed it might be turned to good account. Into the phone he said, 'As a matter of fact we're thinking of going to Playa del Medano, the swimming is very safe there.'

'The boy also?'

'I think not.'

'Then, señor, if you were to telephone me from Medano it might be the . . . strategic moment for me to

give you the news that Señor Hunter's body has been
found.'

'Yes indeed. We shall probably have lunch at the
hotel.'

'I suggest you warn the ladies that the corpse is in a
considerable state of disrepair. I think you can dissuade
them from wishing to see it.'

'Yes.'

'I shall be at the police station in Las Rocas at twelve-
thirty. May I expect your call between then and one
o'clock?'

'Certainly. Thank you for your trouble, Lieutenant.'

'Thank you for your co-operation, señor.'

MacAlistair rejoined the others on the terrace.
Catherine Hunter looked up at him. 'No news?'

'I'm afraid not, just a routine call. I must say he's very
efficient.' Out of the corner of his eye he could see that
David had untangled the line and was now rewinding it.
He judged this the correct moment to ask, breezily,
'Okay—how about Medano?'

Catherine said, 'Shouldn't we be here, in case the
police need us?'

'I can always call *him*, just to check. And I don't think
you should sit around this house.'

Anne thought that Medano would be nice; she meant
that looking at MacAlistair in his swimming-trunks would
be nice. David said, 'Not me, thanks all the same, I'm
going to catch our supper.' He swung his legs over the
wall, judged the distance, and dropped on to the dry
crumbling earth beyond. Lizards skittered in all
directions, nearby cicadas paused for a second and then
recommenced their endless susurration.

Catherine Hunter called out, 'David, you will be
careful?'

'Of course.'

'If we're out, what about lunch?'

'I'll raid the fridge.'

'Don't forget.'

'I won't.' He was already walking away from them towards the ocean.

Lieutenant Dominguez and Patrick MacAlistair were not the only people prepared on that day for the discovery of Alex Hunter's body. Morales and Acton, adding up the facts at their disposal, could hardly doubt that something of the sort was about to happen, even if the more arcane details were denied them. For this reason Acton had taken up only a temporary position above the villa, and Morales had put a Spanish press card in his pocket before repairing to the bar opposite the police station.

Acton found a reasonably shady spot just off the main road from which he could see the house without getting out of his car, an improvement on the fly-infested jungle of the previous afternoon. He watched David Hunter loping down the hill towards the rocks, and quickly ascertained through the binoculars his purpose there. When, half an hour later, MacAlistair drove away in the Mercedes, mother and daughter again inside it, Acton, as before, could observe most of their progress towards the main road where they turned towards Los Christianos. Presently he followed; even Morales had agreed that there was no point in watching an empty villa; but it was interesting, perhaps vital on this particular day, to know that Alex Hunter's son had again stayed at home.

The wide beach at Medano was not crowded. Catherine Hunter, her daughter, and MacAlistair took a swim in the shallow water, then lay in the sun.

Catherine was aware of Anne's muddled yearning towards MacAlistair. Poor child! fifteen was a dreadful age. The mother in her found it strange that a second generation should be under the spell of those clean-cut

American good looks, not to mention the powerful body which had changed so little over the years. (Come to think of it, he and Alex had been alike in this respect, and yet one had never been aware of them jogging, playing tennis, working-out, indulging in any of the keep-fit antics which so obsessed other men. Strange!) The woman in her could not help recalling that single, interesting and frustrating, occasion when he had made a grab for her: so very much too late in the day.

Years before, meeting Patrick and Alex together at a baseball match near Frankfurt where they, as well as her father, were stationed, MacAlistair was the one in whom she'd been interested but Alex was the one to show interest in her; Patrick seemed unaware of her existance. This was why she had been so startled by David's sudden question, 'Do you like him?' and this was why, as far as she was concerned, their later passage-at-arms struggling on her sofa had been the completion of a circle. Alex, forever absent, had pushed them apart in an ironical repetition of their first meeting.

Now Alex was dead, no longer able to wound; and out of all the past, what should return to haunt her, nagging and nagging at her damned Matheson conscience, wearing her down until even her son noticed it, but her one and only affair, not with Patrick who had always attracted her but with a meaningless young man encountered at a meaningless cocktail-party? She could barely remember his face.

At the time, certain that Alex was being unfaithful to her in Hong Kong or Athens or wherever that particular absence had taken him, she probably felt that she was 'getting her own back'. Not that she would have accepted this as a motive; if there'd been a motive at all it lay within the treacherous body which needed Alex and, Alex failing it, took whatever was available — but not Patrick!

Most of her women-friends passed through similar

lapses; and if *their* husbands had ever disappeared for five weeks, let alone five months, it would have been a matter of divorce. Well, it so happened that she was different; but why did the memory of that single casual affair persecute her now? Could it be because she had never confessed it to Alex, just as she had never completed the trifling argument which had been their last conversation? And how stupid, how criminally stupid of her not to realize until now, when he would never return, how much she had always looked forward to his returns, perhaps subconsciously, and relied upon them. Because she had resented the absences she had failed to understand that they were the pattern of her life, flawed like the pattern of all lives, but, oh God! golden in comparison to this inert finality.

MacAlistair suggested another swim, then lunch. With the habitual courtesy which people mistook for compassion he waited until the meal was nearly over before saying, 'Hey, I forgot — I'd better call Dominguez.'

When he came back to the table Catherine knew immediately from his expression that something had happened. 'It's not . . . They haven't . . . ?'

MacAlistair nodded gravely. 'It was found this morning, quite a long way to the west.'

Anne reached out and took her mother's hand. Catherine, who hadn't known until this moment that something deep inside her had been hoping that her husband was in reality still alive, said, 'I . . . I'm glad. The . . . not knowing . . .' And then, with more conviction, 'Yes, yes. Thank God!'

MacAlistair assumed an embarrassment which he was constitutionally incapable of feeling. 'The police want me to . . . There has to be an identification.'

Catherine Hunter squared her shoulders, every inch a Matheson. 'I'll go now.'

'No.'

She stared at him. He added, more gently, 'It's . . . I wish I could spare you this, Catherine, but the body . . . Well, it's been in the sea two days. Dominguez made a special point; he said, "It would be too distressing for the señora." '

'Oh.' She looked away, squeezing her daughter's hand, pulling herself together. 'Yes, I see. I . . . I'm not very good at that kind of thing.'

'The Lieutenant's perfectly prepared for me to do it. I've known Alex for a long, long time.'

'That's very good of you, Patrick.'

'Nonsense! what am I here for?' Then, in case there should be any soul-searching and concomitant change of mind, he left the table quickly, saying, 'It won't take long, I'll find you on the beach.'

He drove straight to the small hospital in Las Rocas where Dominguez was waiting. His manner indicated that they were now going to play it straight, for the benefit of police underlings and hospital officials. MacAlistair allowed himself to be led upstairs and into a cold grey room where the body, unpleasantly shapeless, lay beneath a sheet.

It was not by any means the first time he had seen a corpse, and one or two had been in worse condition than this, nor indeed the first time he had been called upon to give a false identification. No denying, however, that it was always an unpleasant business; the man, whoever he might have been, had certainly spent some days in the water: rather longer, MacAlistair calculated, than the span of time since Alex Hunter's drowning; but that was a detail, and one which the whey-faced young doctor accompanying them probably didn't have the experience, or the stomach, to judge; at any rate, he appended his signature to the document of identification, with rather a shaky hand, under that of Dominguez and MacAlistair, before pouring them both a glass of Fundador, and a somewhat larger one for himself; medicinal purposes.

After he had withdrawn, Dominguez said, 'I let word slip out, before I left Santa Cruz. From my point of view, regarding the tourists, we need a little publicity.'

'Of course.' It had been part of the deal.

'They'll be waiting downstairs.' On the way he explained that his tiresome superior had been delighted that the matter was now cleared up. 'The first time I've seen him smile for at least a year, señor. I believe he has almost forgotten how to do so.'

Morales was standing among the fifteen or so people in the entrance to the hospital; of these only three were connected with the press; the others comprised a passing doctor, a nurse, a cleaning woman, a porter with a trolley of soiled linen, a party of visitors transfixed by curiosity, a couple of policemen. Morales had prudently positioned himself so that he belonged to no particular group; if questions were asked there was always the press card. He hadn't expected Dominguez to be accompanied by MacAlistair but was definitely not surprised to see him at the Lieutenant's side. This then was the eventuality of which he had said to Acton, all unknowing, 'You're still clean with the Hunters as long as he's not around, and I'm still clean with him as long as they're not around.' Naturally he had surmised, ever since seeing the sign 'mortuary' in Santa Cruz, that Mrs Hunter would not be called upon to view the corpse.

Dominguez now made a concise statement: he was relieved to be able to report that the body of Señor Alexander Hunter had been found near Punta de la Tixera, this side of San Juan. Doctors had verified that the cause of death was drowning; there was no evidence of foul play. Señor Patrick MacAlistair, the dead man's friend for more than twenty years, had identified the body without hesitation, thus saving the grieving widow from that gruesome task. He went on to stress that all

beaches safe for swimming were clearly marked, and he
hoped that the gentlemen of the press would once again
urge their readers to make sure, before taking any risks,
that they were in a safe area. He thanked them all very
much — were there any questions . . . ?

There were half a dozen desultory questions, but
Morales didn't even hear them, he was too busy thinking.
He had been ordered to get 'definite verification' of Alex
Hunter's death, and it had suddenly struck him that in
spite of every indication to the contrary the body lying
somewhere in the depths of the hospital might in fact *be*
that of Alex Hunter; as things stood at the moment he
couldn't report with absolute certainty that it was and he
couldn't report that it wasn't; and he obviously couldn't
afford to make a dangerous mistake either way, the very
idea chilled his blood. If the identification had been
phoney, as all the evidence suggested, the corpse would
be extremely well guarded, and Morales hadn't a hope in
hell of verifying his suspicions. But wait a minute . . . !

The little crowd was now dispersing; MacAlistair and
Dominguez were climbing into the latter's car; in a few
seconds Morales would be alone, and conspicuous.

Yes, of course! There was a way. Only one person
capable of telling them the truth would be allowed to see
Alex Hunter's body. The move would have to be made
very fast indeed, but it looked as if luck, with a strong
push from Acton's prescience, was going to be on their
side.

15

At about the time that Dominguez ushered MacAlistair
into his borrowed office at the tiny police station of Las
Rocas, gesturing as he did so towards the tape-recorder

which already reposed on a desk, David Hunter, searching the villa's refrigerator for something to eat, heard the telephone ringing in the living-room.

Acton's voice said, 'Oh, it's you. Family around?'

'No, they're out.'

'Did you know they've found your father's body?'

Shock and anger hit David simultaneously. 'Why the hell didn't they tell us?'

'They told your friend, Mr MacAlistair.' In his role of journalist he began to describe the scene at the hospital, as relayed by Morales. David listened, anger growing; Acton had found exactly the right note of callous irony with which to feed it. 'The thing is, you may be right not to trust him.'

'MacAlistair? Why?'

'Of course it could all be bullshit, you know what people are like, but there's a story going around that it wasn't your father's body at all.'

'Jesus Christ! why would Patrick . . . ? But wouldn't the police . . . ? Dominguez must have . . .' Acton let him flounder about in this morass for a while, knowing that his thoughts, allied to his dislike of MacAlistair, would produce more explosive results that any words. David was seeing, in his mind's eye, the reflected drink poured over the wall of the terrace, the reflected glance of amusement, of contempt, which had passed between the two men. 'What the hell's going on?'

'Search me! Why don't you come over to Las Rocas and see for yourself?'

'By God, I will—that's exactly what I'll do.'

'Got a car?'

'Yes. They went in MacAlistair's.'

'Know the hospital?'

'Yes.'

'Meet you there in, what? twenty minutes. Oh! and you'd better bring your passport, you may need to prove who you are.'

As David ran out of the villa, MacAlistair was listening to the third of six taped conversations which Dominguez had selected for his attention. And this was the one, no doubt about that! The situation was complicated by the fact that he had no idea how much the tape was going to reveal or how much of it Dominguez could understand. One half of his mind was assessing exactly what these voices meant to him personally, the other half was trying to guess what they might mean to a Spanish policeman.

Of course he had never seen Morales, not consciously, and he had never heard his voice, but he knew that he wasn't listening to 'Andrew Castle', therefore the chances were that this was 'Señor Serrano'. As for the voice from London, he would have recognized it anywhere and could even attach facial expressions to accompnay the words of the white-haired young man with the moustache who called himself Peter: 'Hello, Johnny! Having a good time?'

'Smashing. The sea was a bit rough this afternoon, so we couldn't go swimming, but Eddie went for a walk along the rocks with young Martin.'

'I expect that was interesting.'

'Yes. Martin told him he doesn't like Jennings; doesn't trust him.'

'Poor old Jennings!'

'Might come in handy.'

'Poor old Jennings' could translate all this as easily as Peter could—thank God they weren't using a proper code! So David Hunter had gone for a walk with 'Eddie', had he? Yesterday afternoon, when 'poor old Jennings' had escorted his mother and sister up to the cool slopes of El Tiede. 'Eddie' was therefore 'Andrew Castle'. Note that David had never mentioned seeing him again— significant.

In this manner, MacAlistair listened to a detailed report of all their activities on the previous day. He wasn't

sure about the Lieutenant's English; did he for instance
realize that he himself was 'Denis' and that 'Señor
Serrano' had followed him to Santa Cruz, witnessed a
meeting there, shadowed his colleague to a hospital — to
the door of the mortuary? He hoped that his own
expression revealed nothing, but a cold sweat was
creeping on his back. They knew; they knew everything!
But there was worse to come: the voice from London said,
'Good! Glad you're having a nice holiday. How's Joanna?'
   Shock prevented MacAlistair from hearing the answer.
Joanna was still *here*!

David Hunter parked the Volkswagen, which went with
the villa, in a fashion as unruly as his emotions, and
jumped out; he couldn't remember having been so angry
in his entire life, and he was too young to recognize within
the anger, powering it like the catalyst in a reactor, a
small pellet of fear. Acton coming forward to meet him,
and Morales watching from behind a newspaper in his
car, both recognized the anger with satisfaction.
   Acton said, 'Look, it may be just a rumour, all balls.'
   'Soon find out. Anyway, why was MacAlistair told and
not me?' He ran up the steps and into the entrance hall. A
Sister turned towards him enquiringly. David said, 'My
name is David Hunter. I understand the body of my
father is here — Alexander Hunter who was drowned. I
wish to see it.'
   This was the beginning of the countdown; Acton knew
that from this moment there would be a limited, and alas
incalculable, number of minutes before Dominguez was
summoned and came running. MacAlistair might well be
with him, and Acton could not afford to be seen again by
MacAlistair, least of all in the present situation.
   The Sister was dithering; the doctor on duty was being
summoned. David had remembered to bring his passport
as instructed; he was holding it in one hand and hitting it

with the other. Too bad about the time factor. How long
would the doctor take to appear? Was he likely to be in on
the deception or merely another patsy?'

He appeared, looking perplexed. Either he was a very
good actor, many doctors were, or he was straight, Acton
thought the latter. David was banging his passport again
and shouting in his distressing Spanish, 'I am the son of
my father, I should have been called immediately, I shall
report this matter to the British Consul.'

The doctor said, 'Allow me to speak to the department
concerned. A moment, please.' The moment was a long
one; Acton was getting fidgety, one ear attuned to the
signal which Morales would give when he saw the police
car approaching: two quick toots of the horn if
Dominguez was alone, three if MacAlistair was with him.

It was arranged. The doctor was saying, 'I apologize for
this upsetting circumstance, señor. I can't imagine why
you were not informed, the matter will be investigated.'
He gestured towards a staircase. Acton whispered to
David, 'I'll be outside. Don't forget to let me know.' David
nodded, grim-faced, already beginning to look more
scared than angry. He followed the doctor upstairs.
Acton turned quickly out of the building and ran to join
Morales who had parked his car in a more strategic
position, half-hidden behind an ambulance.

MacAlistair was now thanking Dominguez for having
taped the telephone calls. To his relief he had realized
that the policeman's command of English was
rudimentary; and if in the future curiosity prompted him
to have the conversations translated they would mean
little or nothing to him, lacking as he did key-knowledge
of the individuals concerned.

'But they were of value to you, señor?'

'Yes. I understand it all now. These men wish to obtain
Señora Hunter's interest in our business; they wish to do

so behind my back. I can't thank you enough.' It wasn't
very good but it would have to do; in any case, he guessed
that Dominguez was more interested in his own
promotion than in the possible meaning of any telephone
call.

At this point the policeman whom Dominguez had
detailed to guard the corpse succeeded in getting through
to his commanding officer. The Lieutenant listened,
snapped 'Wait!' covered the mouthpiece, and said to
MacAlistair, 'The Hunter boy is at the hospital
demanding to see his father's body.'

MacAlistair stood up. He was interested, as always, to
notice that his reflexes were functioning correctly. 'Your
man can't stop him, of course.'

'No.'

'We'd better go at once.'

Dominguez told his subordinate to take no action,
slapped down the receiver and ran out of the room,
MacAlistair close behind him.

The doctor turned to David and said, 'Señor, you will find
this a distressing experience. The body is not . . . entire
and has been in the sea some time.'

David faltered. Anger had evaporated; he now felt only
fear and repugnance—and determination, after all he
was in part a Matheson. He said, 'I'm ready.'

He wasn't. The smell was nauseating, and the shapeless
lump under the sheet almost too horrible to contemplate.
He didn't want the sheet to be lifted; it was lifted. There
was no head to speak of, portions of skull gleamed
through what remained of the flesh. The right arm was
missing; whole areas of the torso were hideously
lacerated, by rocks presumably, and in places
decomposed.

Finding a shred of voice, David said, 'Please turn it . . .
him over.' Then he remembered that it had to be said in

Spanish; he managed, 'Turn, please.'

Beneath his father's left shoulder-blade there had been three small moles set in an irregular triangle. The body was turned with difficulty; the area in question was not lacerated, not even bruised, and of course there were no moles.

David reeled away, covering his mouth with his hand; the doctor seemed to be offering support, but David shook his head, wondering all the same what had happened to the bones of his legs. The door of the hideous grey room was wavering to and fro, he would never reach it.

The police car jerked to a halt. MacAlistair and Dominguez erupted from it and ran into the hospital. Watching, Acton snickered, and Morales remained silent. A great deal now hung in the balance.

On the staircase, MacAlistair said, 'Leave this to me, I must talk to the boy alone.'

'Of course.'

Thus David, tottering out of the appalling grey room, found himself face to face with his father's best friend and business partner; he didn't even notice Dominguez who had netted the doctor, the policeman on duty, and the mortuary attendant, sweeping them all silently out of the way.

David walked past MacAlistair to an open window and leaned there, gulping fresh air. He didn't think he would ever be able to rid himself of that sickly-sweet, sour stench. MacAlistair was silent, reflexes all on tiptoe, poised; he eyed the boy with intense professional acuity.

'It's not . . . not Father.'

'I know.'

'Then why the hell did you say it was?'

Barely twenty-four hours ago, sitting on Catherine Hunter's bed, MacAlistair had foreseen the dim shape of

an eventuality which might compel him to take Alex's son
into his confidence, even though he knew that by doing so
he would put the boy in danger. The decision he had to
make now, immediately, within the next sixty seconds,
was the degree of truth demanded of him at this moment.
He looked out of the window at the huddled rooftops of
Las Rocas. Somewhere under one of them was Joanna,
and he'd better not forget it!

'Who put you up to this, David?'

'Answer my question first. Why did you say . . . ?'

'The man you think is called Andrew Castle?' Not too
difficult a guess after listening to that telephone
conversation, but David was taken aback. Before he
could open his mouth to deny it, MacAlistair said, 'He
put you up to it, and he asked you to tell him right away
whether or not that—' jerking his head towards the
terrible grey room—'is really your father. I suppose he's
waiting outside for an answer.'

This omniscience aroused what was left of David's
anger; it didn't make a very good showing. 'He's not the
only one I'm telling. I'm going to show you up, I'm going
to . . .'

'You don't know what you're talking about, Davey.'

'Don't Davey me!'

'I said it was your father's body because he's still alive,
I'm trying to protect him, don't you understand?'

What David understood was that this statement, with
all its proliferating implications, didn't surprise him as
much as it should; therefore, subconsciously, since it had
never entered into his reasoning, he had already considered it: something to do with the fact that neither
accident nor suicide had made sense, something to do
with those damned reading glasses . . . He felt sick and
dizzy. He thought that he had rearranged the chess-board
to his satisfaction, but here it was tilting and turning all
over again, the pieces sliding about, changing positions,

assuming different shapes. He remembered how intently MacAlistair and Andrew Castle had regarded each other down there on the rocks, how curtly MacAlistair had dismissed the younger man, how . . . Oh God, there were too many things to remember, everything would have to be reassessed yet again, was he going to vomit? He said, 'Then . . . then who *is* Castle?'

'I don't know. If I said I did I'd be lying—but they're your father's enemies.'

'They?'

'He and the phoney insurance guy.'

David shook his head, lost. MacAlistair took him by the arm and held him firmly. 'Look, I'll explain it all, as much as I know. Right now only one thing matters—they *must* be made to think that your father's dead, everything depends on it. You've got to tell them that I was right, that the body *is* his. If you don't, they'll find him and kill him.'

Thus it was that presently David came out of the hospital alone and stood on the steps looking dazed. Acton appeared from among parked cars and beckoned to him. David advanced, and allowed himself to be drawn out of sight behind the ambulance.

'Well?'

David examined the other young man's face, but it hadn't changed, it was as open and friendly as ever. Nothing had changed, yet everything had changed. He was surprised how easy he found it to say, 'It's my father all right.'

If Acton was surprised he didn't show it. 'Where's your friend MacAlistair?'

'In there—signing things. We . . . we have to take the body home.'

Acton nodded. 'Then I dragged you all this way for nothing. Sorry about that.'

'It doesn't matter. Thank you . . . Thank you for being

concerned. I'd better go, they need my signature too.'

He trailed back to the hospital, went in at the door, and then turned to the window where MacAlistair stood, watching. They both saw the Seat drive away and the two men in it. MacAlistair glanced at him. David said, 'Yes, that was Señor Serrano.' He had once walked across a quicksand for a foolish schoolboy dare; the ground had slid and trembled beneath his feet, it was doing the same now. MacAlistair, recognizing the symptoms from bitter experience, put on a hard, practical voice: 'Better move. Your mother will be wondering where the hell I am. You go home, pretend you know nothing, act surprised when I tell you the body's been found and I identified it. Okay?'

'You said you'd explain.'

'I will. Not now, we'll need time.' Time: to think, to sort out fact from fact, lie from lie, danger from danger. Time: glancing at his watch he could hardly believe that only one and a half hours had passed since he'd left Catherine Hunter and her daughter at Medano. Ninety minutes which he, which all of them, would certainly live to regret.

16

Morales and Acton stopped at a tourist hotel, not one they'd used before; they ordered drinks in the cool, deserted bar—the packages were all blistering by the pool—while Morales telephoned London.

'Five-nine-seven-nine.'

'Johnny here.'

'Hello, Johnny, how's Tenerife, having a good time?'

'Wonderful. Arthur just joined us, at least I think his name's Arthur.'

The fat man said, 'Wait a second!' He nodded to a

sandy, unremarkable individual with washed-out blue eyes who was sitting on the far side of the bare modern office behind a bare modern desk. Above his head, almost cancelling him out with its vehemence, hung an abstract painting, crimson and black triangles jangling across a murky background. This person picked up an extension phone and listened. The fat man continued: 'Johnny? You mean you're not sure it *is* Arthur?'

'Not one hundred per cent. Jennings says it is and young Martin agreed with him, but they could be playing games with us.'

The man behind the desk stretched his neck as if his shirt was uncomfortable, it was a habit. Blinking, stretching his neck, he bore an uncanny resemblance to an ancient turtle, even though he was only in his late forties. He said, 'Games!' and covered the mouthpiece of the extension; the fat man did the same. 'If MacAlistair is "playing games", and if he's gone so far as to involve Hunter's son, it's time he was stopped.'

The other nodded agreement; then said into the phone, 'Wait, please, Johnny.'

Morales waited, wondering if the girl on the hotel switchboard, hearing nothing, would take it for granted that the conversation was over and disconnect the line. The minutes crept by. Morales shrugged to himself; *he* wasn't paying for this expensive telephonic silence and, like white-haired Peter, knew better than to interrupt it.

After a long time the fat voice returned. 'Johnny?'

'Yes.'

'Is the line good, can you hear me?'

'Yes.'

'Here's what you do. Get hold of Joanna—tell her this . . .'

17

Even when they were all back at the villa it was a long time before David and MacAlistair could find an opportunity of talking together, at length, in private. The discovery of Alex Hunter's body raised a number of practical questions which could not be discussed too quickly or bluntly. How long would the Spanish authorities delay before releasing the body? Which airline would be most likely to transport it back to England as soon as possible? What arrangements had to be made, both here and there, for its journey? What was the attitude of the medical bureacracy at London airport to this kind of cargo? . . .

Eventually, however, Catherine Hunter and her daughter trailed upstairs to shower and change. MacAlistair nodded to David and they took their drinks out on to the terrace, perched themselves on the low wall and were silent for a while. David was not to know how carefully the older man had considered this ordinary action before taking it, going out on to a terrace and sitting on a wall, nor how courageous it was. Courage imposes its own widely differing standards; the man who reacts with instinctive, often mindless, bravery in an emergency belongs to a very different category from the man who, having considered the matter with care, sits down with a drink in his hand, knowing that at this moment or the next he may well be shot dead.

As far as MacAlistair was concerned, the preparatory silence meant that he was waiting to be killed, there was no point in hiding, and in any case nowhere to hide.

Nor was he far wrong. At that moment Acton was parking his car at the edge of the banana plantation, exactly where he had parked it the day before. He and Morales got out of the front seat; Joanna got out of the back. Acton opened the boot of the Seat, and Joanna reached in, unfolded a costly-looking piece of velvet, which seemed out of place lying next to a rusty jack and assorted tools, took from it a gleaming rifle with telescopic sights and hung it carefully over his right shoulder.

Joanna, or rather 'Joanna', his name was Ernst Weber, was a neat, mousey man of no particular age, something between twenty-eight and forty-eight, with brown hair brushed straight back and mild brown eyes gazing from the kind of characterless face which might confront you over the desk of any minor civil servant. He accepted all instructions without argument, providing that they didn't run counter to his strong feeling on food—he was a strict vegetarian, the kind who will only wear plastic shoes— and guns: he was without question one of the finest marksmen in the world, but unfortunately moved in circles where his prowess was not likely to be put to the test in orthodox competition.

Acton locked the car and led the other two through the shadowy plantation to the far side of it where he had spent the previous afternoon watching the villa. As the vegetation thinned out, the first things the three of them saw were the figures of David Hunter and Patrick MacAlistair sitting side by side on the wall of the terrace like, exactly like, ducks in a fairground shooting-range, not even rotating ones.

Acton said, 'Nice, eh?', but Ernst Weber, expression-less as ever, shook his head. 'Too far. Back light.' Authority had spoken; it gestured to the left where the plantation dropped down the hill in a south-westerly direction, curving a little closer to the house. They drew back under cover of the palms, Weber leading the way.

MacAlistair sighed, sipped his Scotch, said, 'Yes,

well—you're not going to like this, Davey, I wish I didn't
have to tell you.'

David almost wished that he didn't have to be told, but
they were both captives of the situation and could only
escape from it in one direction.

'Do you remember, over a year ago now, your father
went to Italy? Those interesting hand-woven carpets—don't you have one in your bedroom at home?'

'Yes.'

'What you didn't know was that we were in a hell of a
mess at the time. Crises in Europe *and* in the States,
dollar low as hell, pound sky-high and valueless. Small
businesses were going bust left right and centre, and
Artifax was next.'

David realized with a certain sense of shame that none
of these realities had impinged very much on his tight
little world of study and examinations, the occasional
game of squash, occasional disco, occasional girl. He felt
like a child: or rather he felt that at the time, up to a few
days ago in fact, he had *been* a child.

'Your father came back in February. He brought some
of the things with him, we often did, if they were reasonably small and light.'

'The carpets weren't small and light.'

'No, but he'd found a few other pieces, including some
nice inlaid boxes, did you ever see those?'

'I don't think so.'

'He bought seven dozen, we were trying them out in the
States too, and three of them . . .' He stared into his
drink, avoiding David's eye. 'Three of them were the real
thing.'

'Real?'

'Genuine Renaissance. Worth about . . . well,
Sotheby's eventually sold two for forty thousand pounds
each, and the other for seventy-five.' He went on quickly,
while his exact meaning dropped like a stone into David's

already clouded mind. 'Your father's an honest man, Davey, you know that as well as I do — but we were going down for the third time, no more bank loans. And it wasn't just Artifax, he was thinking of your mother, you and Annie at school, you just about to go to college. So he . . . decided to jump on the band-wagon, join the great universal fiddle. In his position I'd have done the same.'

David was shocked by this revelation, but only in so far as his generation could be shocked by anything, nourished as it was on a nightly television diet, both real and fictional, of dishonesty, disaster and violence. The Matheson genes put up a token show of reproach, but even they had been forced to adapt themselves to the times.

'We'd been doing business with this guy in Florence for years. I guess I can tell you his name, but don't repeat it — Andreotti. Rich as hell! Your father happened to tell him how things were, and he . . . he said he'd like to help us. Of course we had no idea there was this other side to his business. He said he'd make it worth our while if Alex imported the three boxes with the rest of our merchandise; he said a Mr Fairweather would call on us in London and collect them. He did — nice unassuming little guy; paid us twenty-five thousand for the three. They went to Sotheby's about six months later, I happened to see a picture of one of them in the paper, "Record Sale", etcetera.'

David was looking at his father's partner with renewed interest. 'So you went on doing it.'

'I didn't — but that doesn't let me out, I'm not pretending it does. Your father said Andreotti trusted *him*, there was no guaranteeing he'd trust me, I might screw the whole deal. So . . .' A gesture. 'He did the importing, I did the receiving, Mr Fairweather did the processing.'

'And Sotheby's took their percentage.'

'It wasn't always Sotheby's — and anyway as far as the auctioneers were concerned the stuff was authenticated, clean. We did it about . . . eight, nine times during the year. Artifax never looked back.'

'Didn't the Customs and Excise people . . . ?'

'We're old friends, Davey, we've been importing since . . . When did we start up? 1968, wasn't it? They trusted us, we were part of the scenery. But then . . .' He finished his drink and put the glass down on the wall beside him. 'Then something went wrong, very wrong.' The voice was bleak suddenly. David drank his beer and waited.

'Maybe I gave you the impression that Andreotti only worked out of Italy. He doesn't, he's the big time. Israel, Hong Kong, Spain, Africa . . . quite an operator!'

'Not drugs too?'

'Oh God no, we'd have drawn the line at that. Just antiques, antiquities, not even phoney ones.' He sighed deeply. 'Early last month your father went to Greece.'

David nodded.

'We've been importing a lot of those statues — kind of semi-repro. They go over big in the States . . .'

'Mother's got one in the hall. Aphrodite.'

'That's correct. The guy's quite an artist, turns out nice stuff, big and small, no junk. Your father was in touch with Andreotti before he left; usual arrangement, a contact-man would call on him at his hotel in Athens. Know anything about Tanagra figurines?'

'I've seen them in museums.'

'That's where most of them are. Tanagra was an ancient Greek town in Boetia. These little statuettes are from the tombs there.'

'Valuable?'

'More or less priceless, the good ones. Anyway this contact-man had two, beauties, our cut seventy-five thousand.'

David grimaced.

'Your father packed 'em up with the rest of the small pieces, air freight, no problem. Mr Fairweather comes around to collect them, nearly has a fit. Fakes!'

'But who . . . ? How . . . ?'

'Who-how's right! Fairweather gets on to Andreotti and the shit hits the fan. By the time it clears everybody's looking at your father.'

'Oh God!'

MacAlistair, grim-faced, glanced at the young man beside him. 'This holiday—pretty sudden, wasn't it?'

'Very.'

'We thought that maybe if Alex could disappear quietly for a while, give Andreotti time to find out what had really happened . . . But it seems that however he added it up, the answer came out the same: the things were handed over to your father in Greece, and somewhere along the way between Athens and London *he* handed them over to the highest bidder—and believe me there'd have been bidders!'

'It wasn't true.'

'Of course not! Somebody knew, somebody fixed him.' He shook his head. 'And it isn't so easy to get away from a guy like Andreotti. I called him in Florence five times, I tried to reason with him, he told me to go screw myself; he said nobody, but nobody, double-crossed Andreotti; he said he had powerful business associates who were pushing him to take action. And when Italians talk about powerful business associates they only mean one thing.'

'The Mob.'

'Right. If it hadn't been for Fairweather . . . *He* didn't believe it was your father, and he warned me—they were sending these guys out to Tenerife to . . . God, it sounded impossible, but of course it wasn't, it happens every day. They were going to grab your father and make him talk— and they have some pretty fancy ways of doing it.'

David's hand was trembling slightly as he put his beer-mug down on the wall.

'I called him right away. I was scared he wouldn't believe me, you know what he's like, but he believed me all right. I told him not to wait, get the hell out of it, and he . . . Don't blame him too much, Davey, he didn't have much time to think. He went swimming and . . . and got drowned.'

'For Christ's sake, why didn't he *tell* us?'

'He will, as soon as he can.'

'*First*! He should have told us first.'

'So they could wire up *your* balls—stub out their cigarettes on your mother's neck? He'd have been putting you all in danger.'

David shook his head savagely, lost for a reply.

'We're dealing with experts, Davey, you've seen 'em in action, you ought to know! The insurance guy had you eating out of his hand. And your good friend Andrew Castle—so interested in whether that was your father's body! I hope to God we fooled 'em, but I wouldn't count on it.'

Morales and Acton were crouching among the banana palms, their eyes on Ernst Weber. He was lying on his stomach behind a pile of rubble where one of the rough drystone walls edging the plantation had crumbled in disrepair; he was aiming the beautiful gleaming rifle; now made an imperceptible adjustment to the telescopic sight. The position wasn't perfect but it was good enough, better than it had been higher up, facing more to the north, less to the west and the setting sun. Had he been interested in anything more human than technique, he could have read the words formed by MacAlistair's lips.

'Davey, he *couldn't* tell you, he didn't dare, don't be so dumb!' He watched the boy struggling with some instinctive disbelief, he was still young enough to possess instincts. 'But he must have known what it would do to

Mother, it isn't like him, he isn't that cruel.'

At this moment, Ernst Weber's finger caressed the trigger lovingly.

It was all very quick, quiet, frightening. David's beer-mug, a couple of feet from his hip, exploded in a glittering shower of glass, the unbroken handle hitting his knee; the sound of the shot seemed incidental. David let out a cry as he jumped up, but MacAlistair had already grabbed his arm in a steely, painful grip. '*Sit down!*'

David obeyed. There was a second's pause during which MacAlistair died three or four times. Then his own glass, not six inches from his body, also disintegrated. The sound of the rifle, not loud, floated lazily up the valley and echoed back from the hillside. Silence.

David said, 'Jesus! what . . .' and ran out of breath.

'Still! Sit still, Davey, don't move!'

In the eternity that followed there was the sound of distant female voices from inside the house. The seconds passed, becoming half a minute. Very slowly MacAlistair relaxed; relaxed his grip on David's arm. He understood.

'What . . . what the hell was that in aid of?' The young man had turned a strange shade of khaki under his tan. MacAlistair, glancing at him, saw that shock had done the trick; the youthful instincts inhibiting belief had been scattered in panic; Alex's son now believed the whole preposterous fairy-tale, the best that MacAlistair had been able to contrive in the short time at his disposal: stolen art treasures, incensed Italian associates, Sicilian hitmen, the works. And all thanks to Joanna's marksmanship—what an irony!

'Patrick, what did it *mean*?'

Female voices getting louder, probably coming downstairs.

'It was a warning.' This at least was the exact truth, shining like the beam of a lighthouse across a complexity of false and treacherous shallows.

'But who . . . ? Why did . . . ? A warning to *me?*'

MacAlistair looked at the ingenuous face, pale in shock. Only the egocentricity and inexperience of youth, he thought, would leap to such a conclusion. For a second he considered using the boy's misinterpretation to his own advantage, and then, discarding the venality as unworthy, said, 'No, not to you—to me.'

'Because you . . . Because it wasn't father's body you identified?'

It was childish, but in the context of his own absurd Italian inventions it would do. 'Yes.'

In fact, he was being warned about so many different things that they defied immediate analysis; particularly in view of the new complications spewed up by the last few hours. However, one thing was certain and required no analysis whatever: this was a turning-point. Even if luck and cunning enabled him to survive, in itself questionable, nothing was ever going to be quite the same again; but then that had been a foregone conclusion for some weeks now, ever since he had lashed himself to the wheel and committed himself to a collision course by helping Alex Hunter.

Alex's wife now came out on to the terrace. 'We thought we heard . . .'

MacAlistair, watched by her son, open-mouthed, was collecting some of the larger pieces of glass. (What the hell kind of bullet could that lethal genius have been using? something of his own invention?) He glanced up and said, 'Sorry I'm such a clumsy ox, I dropped them.'

Next day they left for England. Lieutenant Dominguez had expedited the departure, largely by persuading his superior to use a convenient loophole in the Law. He wanted them all out of the way as quickly as possible: Patrick MacAlistair, the beautiful widow, her son and daughter, and the body of the man who wasn't Alexander Hunter.

PART TWO

LONDON

'Nothing of him that doth fade
But doth suffer a sea-change . . .'

1

'Cavendish Gallery,' announced the poster, 'Abstractions and Deductions by Tom Gerhard'. MacAlistair was gazing at the single Abstraction, or was it a Deduction? which decorated the window against a discreet background of beige velvet. Then he pushed open the door and entered the gallery, glad to escape from London's biting east wind.

A pretty girl with black straight hair looked up at him from her desk and smiled deprecatingly as if she herself didn't think much of Mr Gerhard's efforts. At the far end of the long room a pale couple were whispering with mysterious animation in front of one of the tangled canvases. Looking more closely at a few others, MacAlistair saw that the title of the exhibition made a degree of sense, the paintings did indeed suggest a kind of absent-minded mathematics.

Under cover of this critical scrutiny he soon discerned the closed-circuit television camera which was observing him, hidden in what at first glance appeared to be an air-conditioner over the door. He wondered who exactly was on the receiving end, what comments they were at this moment making.

To say that he felt afraid would not have been the whole truth; in any case he was probably too inured to danger to feel quite at ease without it. Just as his reflexes had reacted appropriately to the disastrous news that David Hunter was demanding to see his father's body, or to the elegant marksmanship which had blasted his whisky-glass but not, for the time being anyway, his body, so they now reacted to the present situation; processed it, bided their time and conserved their energies. He had done all possible thinking, second-guessing, planning, and his mind was now ticking over quietly, prepared to jump in any direction.

The girl finished murmuring into one of the telephones on her desk, stood up and approached him. 'Mr MacAlistair?'

'Yes.'

'Mr Hausner will see you now.'

He noticed that she had been given specific instructions not to escort him to the office; she ushered him through a door behind her desk and into the dingy passage beyond it. After the unostentatious luxury of the gallery this passage had a tatty, uncared-for squalor: a contrast which was, in MacAlistair's opinion, the very essence of London W.1. itself.

As soon as he opened the door he thought, 'Oh-ho, a court martial!' He was aware of his nerves tingling in anticipation, and he also thought, not for the first time, that he had to be some kind of weird pervert to get even the mildest kick out of the danger which was now confronting him. At the desk, under the deplorable painting of black and crimson triangles proliferating on mud, sat Lorenz himself, pale eyes fixed in a stare, scrawny neck forever strangled by his shirt collar. To the right, lounging, or trying to lounge in a chair which was too small for the purpose, was Eddie Amparo, fat face betraying by its particular shade of olive that he was feeling the cold — serve him right for living eternally in the upper seventies Fahrenheit! To the left, leaning against

the wall—did he never sit down?—was Peter Keach,
wearing a grey suit for a change, instead of the macho
leather jacket and tight jeans to which he was addicted;
the suit went nicely with his prematurely white hair and
moustache but, to the trained eye at least, didn't entirely
hide the fact that he was also wearing a gun.

Messrs 'Castle' and 'Serrano' sat side by side on an
expensive leather sofa, the latter self-possessed, the
former uneasy—in the presence of such exalted company
no doubt. The sixth member of the tribunal was
unknown to MacAlistair though the face was familiar,
from photographs perhaps: something military about
him, correct: correctly dressed, barbered, mannered—he
even stood up to shake hands when Lorenz introduced
him: 'I don't think you know George Willingdon.'

Ah yes, Willingdon. Harvard and Oxford, then the
Navy and some undercover connection with the old CIA
in the days before its balls had been cut off to gratify the
high moral precept of American democracy. In the
ensuing shuffle, Willingdon had ended up in what was
officially known, if it was known at all, as the Foreign
Advisory Committee to the Office of the Secretary of
State. This subsection within a subsection not only gave
an impression of being excessively boring but ground out
a mass of stultifying information to prove the point, and
its offices in Washington, where Big is Best, were risibly
insignificant. A committee, for God's sake, not even a
department!

A few people knew its more realistic but equally
theatrical name of Group R Control. This organization
not only kept a profile so low as to be unrecognizable, it
also took the wise precaution of recruiting a high
percentage of its personnel from the countries in which
they were to operate. Lorenz, like Alex Hunter, was
British; Amparo, like MacAlistair himself, American;
Keach some kind of mid-Atlantic Irishman, Acton a

Londoner, Morales a Spaniard. Thus the network was flexible, multi-lingual, camouflaged.

MacAlistair, an old hand at such games, guessed that Willingdon was Group R's gentlemanly troubleshooter extraordinary, and thus more important in the present situation than Lorenz. He decided that a sensible ploy, as well as an amusing one (amusing! he *had* to be insane!) would be to address all his remarks to Willingdon, virtually ignoring the others.

Lorenz, 'Mr Hausner', owner of the gallery, extended the turtle's neck, retracted it again, and said, 'Well, Mac, I suppose we'd better start at the beginning.'

MacAlistair thought, 'Which beginning?', but nodded vague agreement and waited for Lorenz to pick one. The one he picked was tricky, but then he was a tricky bastard, never to be underrated; cruel too. 'At what point did you actually *know* that your friend, Alex Hunter, had disobeyed a direct order, run amok?'

Looking at George Willingdon, MacAlistair replied with surprise and a touch of impatience, 'When you called me into this office and told me about it.'

'Are we expected to believe that he didn't tell you himself, or you didn't guess?'

'I was taught not to guess. Basic training.' This went down well with Willingdon who was the same age and had very likely undergone somewhat the same basic training. 'As for what I expect you to believe . . .' He hoped he had managed to give the impression that in his opinion this was an amateurish way of phrasing a question. It was never wise to antagonize Lorenz, but he had thrown wisdom to the wind nearly three weeks ago.

'Very well, let us accept the premise—temporarily,' Lorenz had at one time been professor at a minor university; sometimes it showed. 'I spoke to you nine days after Hunter had gone on holiday; I imagine we're correct in assuming that you called him in Tenerife and warned him that he was in danger, that we were sending Joanna to kill him.'

'No, you're not correct,' said MacAlistair to Willingdon. 'For three good reasons. One—how could I have known that you were sending Joanna? It must have been a top-level decision and you'd have made damn sure it never reached me. Two—even if I was clairvoyant, do you honestly think I'm that kind of boy-scout? Three—you already *know* I didn't warn him, or it wouldn't have been just a whisky-glass that got shot.'

'Not necessarily. Patrick MacAlistair alive is much more useful than Patrick MacAlistair dead.'

'I hope so.'

'I'm sure of it.' Soft, pale menace.

Perhaps because of MacAlistair's eyes fixed on him, George Willingdon now felt compelled to speak; he spoke rationally: 'Alex Hunter was a close personal friend of yours for more than twenty years, it wouldn't have been unreasonable if you'd thought of him first, us second.'

'Not unreasonable, just treasonable—and stupid. Alex and I agreed, right from the beginning, that if it ever came to the crunch friendship would have to go overboard.'

Eddie Amparo stirred heavily in his uncomfortable chair. 'Bullshit! You warned Alex to get the hell out, and you proved it when you made that phoney identification of the body.'

To Willingdon, MacAlistair said, 'I didn't warn him.'

'Oh sure!' Amparo laughed, fat quaking. 'Now tell us it *was* his body you identified!'

To his surprise, MacAlistair found that he could now afford to play, not exactly an ace, his skimpy hand didn't run to aces, but something good enough to trump the opening trick. With just enough scornful impatience he replied, 'Of course it wasn't his body.'

'So you warned him,' said Amparo, startled by the

admission but not showing it, 'and then you covered up for him.'

MacAlistair sighed. 'For the third and I hope last time, Eddie, I didn't warn him.'

'But you *were* covering-up.'

'Sure I was covering up.' He allowed the fat man a gleam of triumph before adding, 'For *you*, isn't that obvious?' Did you want the Spaniards to know what was going on? They'd have asked every damn question in the book—press, television—at government level, at United Nations level, for Christ's sake! And you had *Joanna* in there too!'

'No, no, no!' Willingdon dismissed these appalling possibilities with a wave of the hand; dismissed fat Eddie Amparo with a look which silenced him for several minutes. 'Whatever your motive—' he let this sink well in—'the positive identification was an absolute necessity, don't think we're not grateful for it.'

MacAlistair had taken the trick, he was careful to show no satisfaction. He noticed Amparo's blubbery lips moving soundlessly, and guessed that he was saying, 'Grateful, shit!'

Willingdon continued, 'As to whether you warned him or not, I think we have to take your word for it that you didn't.'

'Oh,' said Lorenz softly, delicate lids covering pale eyes, 'I don't think we have to take his word for anything. We can easily get at the truth if we want to.'

There was silence. In all his planning and second-guessing MacAlistair had been unable to unearth one good reason why they should really need the answer to this question. So Alex Hunter had learned from some unknown source that they intended to kill him—for God's sake, he could even have guessed it; he was expecting death, he knew that from their point of view he had asked to die; the source of the information was irrelevant. So

MacAlistair had reasoned; but now, in this silence, a terrible doubt assailed him: was there something he had overlooked? A contingency so obvious that it had never entered his head?

He was not lacking in courage, and he seemed to have an insane partiality for danger, but pain was another matter altogether; he wasn't good at it, he dreaded it, and Lorenz knew all there was to know about the infliction of pain. He hoped that his expression had not changed by one iota, because however skilful he might be, these men were his peers: and the two on the sofa, though not in the same league, were coming along nicely. Six pairs of seeing eyes, six finely tuned sensibilities adept at sensing an evasion, detecting a falsehood.

At all costs the face must be kept mobile, the body relaxed; there could be no escape into movement, however expertly simulated: a sneeze, a rearrangement of the legs, could condemn by implication. Basic training. But did they really want the answer, did it matter to them?

'It doesn't matter to us,' Willingdon said, 'whether Hunter was warned or whether he guessed . . .'

MacAlistair breathed again, but covertly; he even shifted in his chair, crossing one ankle over the other.

'. . . What matters is that MacAlistair is going to *find* Hunter for us.'

'You think I can?'

'We think,' said Lorenz, 'that you will—because you have to.' Another darting threat, quick as a snake's tongue.

'And,' added Willingdon, 'since friendship went overboard at the crunch . . .' He smiled. 'By the way, what *was* the crunch?'

The question ignited a quick flare of excitement inside MacAlistair; instinctively, before he'd even had time to consider, he recognized it as an opening which might enable him to trump yet another trick, and an important one, with yet another weak card. 'The crunch?' He allowed himself to consider the question with apparent uncertainty. 'I guess it came when I first realized he wasn't drowned.'

'And when was that?'

'Difficult to say. I saw our friend here — Mr Castle . . .' He waited, making them work, deflecting their concentration.

Lorenz said, 'His name's Acton.'

'I saw our friend Acton talking to David Hunter by the sea, and I . . . yes, that's when I got an inkling — it takes one to know one.'

Peter Keach straightened up from the wall so that the shape of his gun disappeared altogether. He said, 'There was a slight miscalculation here, we were acting on faulty information; MacAlistair arrived earlier than expected or he'd never have seen Acton at all. We were having to move pretty fast anyway.'

Amparo broke his silence by saying, nastily, 'You're trained to move fast.' Keach smoothed his moustache and kept quiet.'

Willingdon ignored these internecine details: 'But when was the actual crunch?'

MacAlistair moved in for the kill. 'I guess it grew slowly. I checked on these boys and found they were using phoney identities . . .'

Amparo sat up in his chair; Keach was looking the other way. MacAlistair struck: 'I made certain arrangements and intercepted one of their phone-calls to London . . .'

Amparo exploded: 'Plain language word-code! *He intercepted one of your reports!*' Keach had paled visibly.

To MacAlistair, Willingdon said, 'I'd always heard you were quite an operator. Then?'

'One of the code-names was Joanna . . .'

'Jesus!' shouted Amparo. 'Why the hell wasn't it changed?'

'And that was the crunch all right. If Joanna was in Tenerife and Alex had died by *drowning*—hell, yes, then I knew he'd made a getaway.'

MacAlistair seldom played poker and was bad at it, but experts had told him that every game reaches a point at which chance or luck or skill suddenly point to the likely winner. He had a feeling that by some fluke, given his lousy hand, he was the one who was into this winning streak. He'd diverted Amparo, Keach, and the two field-men directly involved, by revealing that he'd had access to one or more of their telephone calls, and at the same time gained Willingdon's admiration; under cover of this he'd consolidated the most important of his lies in the best possible manner—by inference, not directly. Only Lorenz remained unmoved in any way, pale eyes rapt in concentration. Had he noticed the legerdemain? Apparently not, because he extended his neck, resettled his collar, and didn't speak. But appearances were never to be trusted where Lorenz was concerned; neither were silences.

Willingdon had opened a folder and was intent on whatever it contained; MacAlistair understood that he was waiting for Lorenz to take the next step forward. Eddie Amparo had settled back, wedged into his chair; occasionally he shot vitriolic glances at Keach who was once more leaning against the wall, whistling silently and gazing at the ceiling. The boys on the sofa sat side by side thinking their own thoughts, uninvolved; MacAlistair had been in their position himself, years ago, and knew that they had been remorselessly questioned before he made his appearance.

Lorenz said, 'In view of the attitude you've chosen to adopt, it would be pointless to ask if you know where Alex Hunter is now.'

MacAlistair recrossed his feet and said nothing; he had been taught to answer questions, not statements. Lorenz was thus forced to add, '*Do* you know?'

'No. How should I? Only a fool would tell me, and Alex isn't a fool.'

'On the contrary, he's the ultimate fool, but that's no business of ours. We have to find him, quickly. How would you go about it, MacAlistair?'

'It would take months. Briefing liaison all over the world, description, photographs — waiting for leads — chasing after dozens of false ones . . . What do I mean, months? It could take years.'

'Quickly.'

'There's no such thing as quickly in that kind of operation, ask anyone who's done it, ask these boys.' He indicated the sofa, Amparo, Keach. He knew that he was telling Lorenz that as far as he, MacAlistair, was concerned Lorenz was an amateur, because he had never worked in the field, suffered all that annihilating routine, the boredom, the frustration; he had come swanning in from his university via various obscure corridors of power.

Willingdon closed his folder with a gentle snap, putting an end to this bickering; he said, 'Alex Hunter was seen arriving at Vienna airport the day before yesterday.'

MacAlistair, recovering from his own shock, did not immediately realize that the information had also shocked every man in the room: which meant that the matter had not been discussed before his arrival; it was the trouble-shooter's way of slapping all these inefficient underlings across the face, it was the tiger dropping its polite Washington mask for an instant to reveal the incisors. He was beginning to like Mr George Willingdon.

Amparo was gaping, Peter Keach's silent whistle was frozen on his lips, the boys on the sofa had turned into mice; Lorenz was giving Willingdon a washed-out stare which, to his credit, expressed absolutely nothing; the thin voice said, 'That's interesting.' His eyes slid across the room to MacAlistair. 'So *now* what action would you take to bring him in? Quickly!'

MacAlistair could afford to play for time because Willingdon's bombshell had put them all in the position of playing for time, Lorenz in particular. 'Vienna. Well, that makes sense, doesn't it? You could almost say, "Where else?" ' he guessed that this remark could only increase their sense of insecurity. For a number of reasons, the most important unknown to anyone in the room but himself, Alex would have been mad *not* to have chosen Vienna. He added, 'Who saw him?'

The question, as anticipated, took them by surprise. Lorenz was deferring to Willingdon, and Willingdon decided upon discretion: 'I don't think it's to anybody's advantage for me to disclose that right now.' He meant that he had no intention of disclosing it because it might be to MacAlistair's advantage.

Once again the adrenalin flared through MacAlistair's body. He said, 'I just thought it might have been Kurt Heldmann.'

Direct hit! To them it must have seemed uncanny but to him it was simple, because only one man could or would have betrayed Alex Hunter and that man was Heldmann; he wondered whether Heldmann was still alive, and doubted it. The fact was that MacAlistair knew far more about Alex in Vienna than they did, and he also knew why they were afraid of Alex in Vienna; he wondered whether to voice the fear or leave it to Willingdon; decided to leave it.

Willingdon said, 'I don't have to tell you that he may have chosen Austria because he intends to cross the frontier.'

There was only one Frontier in their world, that between East and West, and they all knew that Alex Hunter could cross it any time he liked, had already crossed it many times in the course of his duties. Yes indeed, but that was before he had, in Lorenz's phrase, 'run amok'. Now he was at best a madman and at worst a traitor, and in either capacity he might cross The Frontier forever, taking with him a treasure-chest of secret information.

Lorenz looked at MacAlistair and, at his most biting, said, 'Since your friend of twenty years never seems to have confided a single one of his thoughts to you, I won't ask whether *you* think he's contemplating a journey eastwards. Personally I doubt it. I think he's chosen Vienna because he knows it inside out, speaks fluent German, and because it's a city of back doors. That being so, perhaps you'd be good enough to answer my question — what action would you take to . . . retrieve him?' He knew that MacAlistair, having played for time, had now prepared his answers, but that couldn't be helped.

'For a start we have dozens of contacts. Obviously Alex is well-known. A field-man never has the luxury of planning ahead, and I haven't been to Vienna for some months. Things change quickly . . .' They were listening attentively to all this hot air. MacAlistair knew exactly how and where to contact Alex in Vienna, he had known for a good ten years; and if he'd never told them in ten years he wasn't about to tell them now, no sirree! But this he would tell them, and they'd better make no mistake about it: 'A lot depends on how much freedom you give me. If he suspects that you've got a battalion of back-up men breathing down my neck, I'll never get within a mile of him. He may trust me more than he trusts you, but not much more.'

There was another loaded silence. Lorenz looked at Willingdon, but Willingdon was again engrossed in the file. After a moment Lorenz suggested in his most gentle voice, 'On the other hand he trusts his family entirely, doesn't he? I don't find it difficult to envisage circumstances in which they might play a considerable part in his capture. Under your direction of course.'

2

David Hunter watched the optician examine the small section of lens from his father's reading glasses. He was an elderly Jewish gentleman with fine, fastidious features, and David had felt no obligation to explain his motives; the optician's face implied a philosophy of discretion and disinterest learned over the centuries, the hard way.

He now removed the magnifier from his eye, and said, 'No, it isn't a lens. It's a plain piece of glass, as you thought.

David was about to ask if he was quite sure, but then realized that this was a man who never gave an opinion at all unless he was sure. So that was that! He would be interested to hear what MacAlistair had to say about it; not that he intended to enquire directly, those days were over, nor was he prepared to take MacAlistair's answer at its face value. He was astonished to find how easily he had slipped into the indirect mode and the doubting evaluation, both of which were utterly at odds with his character.

He had respected MacAlistair's instructions to say nothing to his mother: particularly, MacAlistair had implied, in view of Alex Hunter's continuing silence. The silence seemed to his son inexplicable when not contemptible; surely he should long ago have contacted his family, or at least his wife, if he was still alive. The 'if' in his thinking surprised David, but the fact was that still, or again, he didn't trust MacAlistair. Mistrust had taken several days to re-establish itself. The shattering of the two glasses on the terrace had tied in so neatly with the odd story of his father's crooked dealing that only very slowly had he come to the suspicion that there was a missing link, that MacAlistair knew more than he was saying.

All this made painful nonsense of the aftermath of death: cremation of someone else's body, a lot of empty talk about the future of Artifax, possible changes in the family income, possible advisability of finding a smaller flat. Direct by nature, David found this aspect of indirection irritating as well as immoral; and though MacAlistair pretended to agree with him, it was perfectly obvious that he didn't really feel any of it. David could just about bear the world beyond the Looking-Glass as long as the real world remained more substantial; but MacAlistair seemed to be living permanently beyond the Looking-Glass, and there were times when that world seemed to be *replacing* the real world; David didn't like this any better than he liked having to witness his mother's pointless grieving.

Though Catherine Hunter remained just as beauti-ful—more so, since hers were the kind of looks which could be fined-down forever—her son sensed that she was wasting away inside; he had an idea that this was to do with something she had done, or not done, in the past, and therefore if his father was really not dead there was nothing, except this callous and continuing silence, to stop her meeting him and exorcizing the desolation; per-haps even the knowledge that he was still alive would do the trick.

The thought brought David to an abrupt standstill in Piccadilly, hindering the progress of passers-by, bundled up against the January cold. It was wrong, it was all wrong; and as soon as he got home . . . no, as soon as he had spoken once more to Patrick MacAlistair he was going to tell his mother the truth; and if MacAlistair didn't like it he could bloody well lump it.

He realized that several of the obstructed passers-by were staring at him curiously: a suntanned young man

with intent grey eyes and an expression of furious
determination. If they knew, by God if they only knew!
What a hole that knowledge would blast in the vacuum of
their tidy self-contained lives! What a glimpse of the
howling chaos outside! No. Looking at their faces, each
inward-turning on its own problems, David knew that
they wouldn't believe, and even if they did believe they
would swiftly and sensibly seize the nearest rational-
ization. Human beings didn't want to know about the howling chaos, they wanted the vacuum, however constrictive,
because within it they felt sane and safe.

He wondered whether he himself would ever feel sane
and safe again; at the moment it seemed unlikely. Even if
his father reappeared this afternoon he couldn't envisage
the Hunter family as constituting an ordinary domestic
unit on the old pattern: with their flat in Kensington and
their cottage in Dorset, retired grandparents, assorted
relatives, Christmas and summer holidays. Admittedly
Anne had gone back to school, re-entering reality even if
it was on a false basis, but would he himself ever get to
university, ever settle down to the study of the world's
agricultural condition and the many ways in which it
might be improved?

As a matter of fact he was now on his way to Foyle's to
buy a copy of *Malnutrition, The Non-Existent Enemy* by
Raymond Halstead. Perhaps the very act of holding a
nice heavy book, opening it, munching his way through
Mr Halstead's rich pudding of statistics, would bring the
real world back to him. Perhaps. But at best it would be a
schizophrenic and temporary relief, at worst he would be
unable to concentrate at all. He trudged on towards the
bookshop. A month ago, an eternity ago, he would have
found this pursuit of knowledge sublimely reassuring. Not
any more.

Patrick MacAlistair was reminded of a fly which, during the endless tedium of some stake-out, probably a fruitless one, he had watched entrapping itself in a spider's web. It had been a large fly, and the spider had been small; the web was not really strong enough to hold the victim, but the spider had darted out of its lair and had swiftly set about securing the monster with almost invisible bonds: within seconds the fly was neatly parcelled for future consumption.

Lorenz, chief spider for Europe North, with his hench-spiders Amparo and Keach, and George Willingdon, imperial spider extraordinary, were now securing their fly, MacAlistair. The fact that they none of them trusted him anyway, least of all when it came to his old friend and colleague, Alex Hunter, made them examine each strand with special care, testing every millimetre for strength and durability.

Oddly enough MacAlistair himself felt removed from the whole proceeding, as if he was watching it happen to someone else. He didn't even listen very intently to what they were proposing, partly because he knew that Lorenz and Amparo would have to repeat the whole thing when it came to briefing, partly because it was unimportant. So Keach was to organize and direct the back-up team; so the Hunters were to stay at an hotel on the Ring, probably the Bristol or the Imperial, with ten men in pairs surrounding them at a discreet distance, and another ten held in reserve in the 6th or 7th District, near the West Bahnhof where strangers excited little or no interest; so Keach was being told, not in so many words, not in front of the victim anyway, that he personally was responsible for keeping an eye on MacAlistair and could pick as many men as he wished for the purpose: all of them, MacAlistair was sure, as unknown to him as Acton and Morales had been—and all as easy to spot.

Would Joanna be among them? He hoped not; had always disliked the feeling that somewhere, out of sight but never out of range, a pastmaster with a superlative rifle was ready to drill a hole in one's back. However, no need to worry about such details just yet. The point was, and well they knew it, that the absolute centre of all this massing of forces, the single component without which the machine was unable to move, was MacAlistair himself. He alone could make contact with Alex, he alone was in a position to coax the Hunter family into co-operation, he alone could as a result crown all this planning with success or confound it with failure. To begin with he had found himself wondering greatly that they should pin all their hopes to a man they didn't trust; only later did he realize that they were doing so because it was their only chance. And, for a few seconds, he had feared Lorenz's threat of pain! It had never even been on the cards; if a tortured man still possesses his faculties he hates too much, and if he no longer possesses them he's useless anyway.

Of course, like the fly, he was trapped, but that wasn't the end of it; if the spider wished to use the fly to entrap other flies, why then he would have to liberate it, and once liberated the fly would have options. MacAlistair had options; they were all dangerous but they were viable. He and Alex together were a match for all these men and their massed forces circling the Ring or held in reserve near the West Bahnhof—yes, even for Joanna himself; but unfortunately they were not together. He, MacAlistair, was the great imponderable in their plans, and Alex was the great imponderable in his. MacAlistair couldn't know what his old friend was thinking or hoping or planning; in some ways he never had known.

When Alex had told him what he'd done (nine days before Lorenz had summoned him to this room for the official revelation, he was right about that) MacAlistair had been appalled; and just as appalled to discover that he wasn't surprised; nobody in their world ever disobeyed an order, but he realized that in this one individual, man of action and visionary, that dangerous mixture, the possibility had always been lying dormant. The actual scale of the disobedience, embracing betrayal and treason, was breathtaking; the fact that by his own idealistic standards Alex had acted correctly and morally was neither here nor there. Friendship or love, or whatever it was, demanded of MacAlistair an immediate decision, but in the end it turned out to be a decision which, from the logical point of view, he didn't have to make at all, because without his knowing or even desiring it the years appeared to have made it for him. A truly sensible man, and a true professional, would have pulled a gun on Alex and handed him over to Lorenz there and then. The past and their long relationship had decided otherwise; MacAlistair was going to help him.

But MacAlistair *was* a logical man and in a way he resented the situation in which he now found himself. This resentment went back to the beginning; it was firmly rooted in the fundamental differences between them.

MacAlistair came from a grimy town near Pittsburgh, son of a Scottish coalminer and a Polish farmer's daughter, both of whom drank to excess: that is to say to the point where their son and his two sisters spent much of their youth hiding from them in cold alleyways and yards, or in the houses of kindly neighbours. Like many coalminers of his generation, Charlie MacAlistair, when sober, had a deep respect for education and forced his son to it, with a belt if necessary. Later, when the boy realized that education was the escape-hatch, something his father had understood all along, he seized it gratefully with both hands and used it to haul himself from the sinking ship; he worked his way, via coffee-shops, gas stations, supermarkets, through high school and college.

Luckily his sisters took after their mother in her youth and were attractive; they also escaped, into more or less successful marriages, leaving their parents to fight it out alone: until the father fell down dead-drunk in the street, fracturing his skull, and the mother succumbed to cirrhosis of the liver.

War in Vietnam interrupted MacAlistair's education; he quickly volunteered for the Army, recognizing that volition would give him a better chance than conscription; he also recognized that Intelligence, if he could break into it, was the sphere least wasteful of his hard-won learning.

Alex Hunter, on the other hand, came from the green English shires, only son of a small-town doctor and an ex-schoolteacher. Brought up in an atmosphere of devout liberalism, he had been sent to the best schools and the best university that his parents could afford. He studied modern languages for which he had an amazing natural talent. This background not only fostered high-minded ideals but practically demanded them; and as for a career, it was only a matter of the boy choosing what form of service he most wanted to perform for the good of mankind.

But unfortunately for his parents, Alexander Hunter was not merely the sum of their good intentions, though it was their liberal teaching which caused him to take such a dislike to the kind of communism then fashionable at universities; this dislike remained passive until the day that his companions took to the streets, brandishing placards, rousing the rabble, and generally acting as the vanguard of a generation which was presently going to wreak havoc all over the world. Once roused, however, he

attacked them vociferously, as well as the popular heroes
of the times: Guevara, Trotsky, Marcuse, Sartre.

As a consequence of this attitude he was noticed by the
talent-scouts of British Intelligence, which had suffered
from its fair share of pinkies, with many more to come,
and yearned to recruit dedicated anti-communists,
liberal-minded ones if possible; he was interviewed and
found promising; the idea appealed to all that was
romantic and idealistic in him. By now he spoke seven
European languages fluently, which qualified him for a
new unit organized by the Americans, but this
necessitated his joining the Army. He did so. His parents
were shattered, and in a sense never forgave him, not
realizing that in his own secret way he was following their
idealistic pattern; security forbade him to explain
himself; after a while they packed their bags and went to
live in Australia where his Aunt Freda was a leading
figure in the crusade for the rights of aborigines.

In the meantime young Hunter was sent to Germany
where he met young MacAlistair who had achieved his
aim and was to undergo the same course of instruction.

Some people hold that opposites make the best
friends — or lovers or marriage partners — others that
affinity is all. Patrick MacAlistair and Alex Hunter,
American and Englishman, could hardly have been less
alike . . . yet here they were, over twenty years later, still
bound together not only by profession but by deep
personal ties; bound even more closely by the ultimate
extravagance of the idealist which had enmeshed the
realist against his will.

MacAlistair couldn't have said why he was helping his
friend. Logically it was madness, therefore he could only
suppose that the motive was emotional: a foggy area of
soft options where he was always at a disadvantage —
result no doubt of the battlefield which had been his
youth.

They both realized at once that Alex would have to
disappear. The drowning gambit, though conventional,
had proved effective enough in the past, and could be
improved upon by positive identification of a body.
However, one did not swim in England in January; Alex,
as a director of Artifax, was due for a winter vacation (the
organization demanded that any such front, particularly
if it involved a family, should be rigidly maintained), and
the nearest sunshine was in Tenerife, which the Hunters
were known to have visited before. Speed was essential, he
must move before Lorenz heard what he'd done, and that
could be any minute.

They argued that Lorenz, even when he did hear,
would at first be unwilling to believe it. Alex Hunter! One
of the most able, the most loyal . . . ! But this delay would
only be a short one, evidence would be forthcoming, what
would Lorenz do then? He would take immediate action,
and the result of that action would be terminal.

So Alex Hunter had gone on holiday with his family
while MacAlistair stayed in London, attuned like some
seismic detector to the subterranean rumbles which must
come. They came in the form of a too-casual summons
from fat Eddie Amparo, an intelligent man behind the
façade; if MacAlistair had not known what to expect he
would never have guessed the motive for fat Eddie's
oblique questions, most of them seeming to be about
something else anyway. He made sure that he was unable
to answer, but said that he would submerge for a couple
of days and see what he could find out.

He 'submerged' by taking to the air, as prearranged.
He spent the two days loitering at the airport in Tenerife,
having travelled with a passport which was not listed on
Lorenz's records under his name — all his professional life
he had taken the precaution of keeping at least one
unlisted passport in a safe place. On the second day of his
vigil who should walk off the ten-fifteen plane from

London, among a gaggle of tourists, but the one and only Ernst Weber, 'Joanna', carrying a neat little suitcase; the gun had doubtless travelled in a nice, safe, diplomatic bag, as it often did.

MacAlistair telephoned Alex Hunter at once and warned him that he now had a target printed on his head; he then took the next plane back to England: Luton airport for a change, using another passport. Then he resurfaced, gave Amparo a few meaningless answers to the questions he had barely asked, and waited for Catherine Hunter to summon him with news of his friend's death by drowning.

As for the personal, emotional issue regarding Alex's wife and son and daughter . . .

His attention was required in the present. Lorenz was saying, 'This story you told the boy, it amazes me you thought of nothing better.'

'There was no time. And anyway it had to fit in with the facts he already knew.'

'He believed it?'

'Yes.' Just—thanks to Joanna's marksmanship, but there was no point in confusing them with this irony; they were discussing the credibility of the story; Willingdon said what MacAlistair was thinking: 'Why argue? The story was told, we have to go along with it.'

. . . The emotional issue was Alex's business, MacAlistair had been glad it wasn't his. He had been married himself, long ago in the early days, but had soon realized the two fundamental points: firstly that marriage didn't go with the job, it was a loner's job: secondly the old conundrum—he only lusted after women he didn't like. Either he had never liked Helen, merely desired her, or he was beginning to like her; either way the marriage was doomed. He had swiftly given his wife both the reason and the wish to divorce him. Thereafter he had watched the Hunter marriage with fascinated horror: the initial happiness, the fatal begetting of a son and daughter—after that childhood he had been determined to render his own union unproductive—the slow destruction of Catherine by process of erosion and evasion, and of the son and daughter by inevitable absence.

How could Alex Hunter be a husband and father? Alex Hunter didn't even exist. What the hell did he think he was doing to that innocent woman, those nice, dependent kids who, in their own very different situation, reminded him of himself and his sisters?

There had been one fierce row between the two men on this subject, they had nearly come to blows. MacAlistair said that Hunter was a selfish high-minded hypocrite with no regard for the responsibility which he had created and could not, by any possible means, sustain. Hunter said that MacAlistair was an emotional cripple, scarred by the experiences of his youth and therefore jealous of what he himself was too frightened to undertake.

The tension between them on this issue never abated; even added something to their professional inter-dependency. Because this was, had to be, so strong they never discussed the matter again, but there it remained, standing apart from their work, apart from their friendship. And the only time that MacAlistair had seized his friend's beautiful and frustrated wife, intending to possess her, and to hell with Alex, the memory of that fierce argument returned to laugh at him; if he had insisted on going forward, or if Catherine had urged him to it, the memory would doubtless have rendered him impotent too . . .

'You feel,' George Willingdon was saying to him, 'that this is a feasible operation?'

MacAlistair shrugged. 'Yes, why not? As long as Alex hasn't burned his boats.'

'Meaning?'

'Lorenz dismisses the idea of his crossing a frontier. I

can't say I do.'

'Not in the role of a defector.'

'Good God no, absolutely the reverse; he detests communism and always has, but he'd be safe there.'

Lorenz shook his head. 'He's not safe anywhere.'

'Safer. He could even disappear completely.'

'Nobody can disappear completely, it's been proved again and again — unless they're dead. Hunter's *supposed* to be dead but he hasn't disappeared, he's been spotted in Vienna. Only when he's really dead will he disappear. The sooner the better.'

MacAlistair didn't argue; no point in arguing with the truth.

George Willingdon was studying the contents of his file again; he seemed to be reading MacAlistair there: 'You're fond of the family, I believe, so you won't want to see them subjected to *undue* pressure.' He looked up. 'You've been extremely skilful in your handling of the situation . . .'

Which situation, MacAlistair wondered — as he was intended to wonder: the situation in which Alex Hunter had landed him three weeks ago, or the situation which was facing him here and now?

'. . . I hope for your sake that your skill and your luck don't desert you in Vienna.'

Though the room had been heavy with veiled theats ever since MacAlistair had entered it, this one was the final straw. He snapped, 'I hope they don't, for your sake too.'

Of course none of them showed shock or surprise or whatever it was they might be feeling; the six pairs of eyes regarded him blankly, and he thought, They aren't human, they really are not human. But at the very same moment he realized that if this was true he himself wasn't human either.

Presently he was dismissed.

*

When the door had closed upon him, Lorenz and Willingdon exchanged a look. Willingdon said, 'How many games is he playing? Two?'

Lorenz shrugged. 'To my mind he's not in a position to play games, not any more.'

'But your mind isn't his. If we've learned nothing else, we've learned not to try second-guessing him.' Since this highly critical remark elicited no response, he sharpened his tone slightly and added, 'He ran circles around everybody in Tenerife.'

It was characteristic of their world that nobody, either then or later, mentioned the fact that by any human or moral standard, Alex Hunter was something of a hero. Long ago he had been chosen because he was a person of fierce loyalties and ideals; they saw no irony in the fact that they were preparing to kill him because of those very virtues. The oldest rule in their ancient book (passed from hand to hand throughout the centuries down the secret rat-runs beneath the corridors of power) was that once a man had erred he must never again be trusted; his motives, however admirable, counted for nothing. In a pantheon which contained no angels, it was self-evident that nobody could ever be on their side.

Willingdon said, 'Well—for better or worse we're stuck with him, but it's a risk; he's a shrewd operator.'

Lorenz shrugged again. 'We're certainly stuck with him. However, I think the risk, though real, is limited; he's a shrewd operator but fundamentally a weak man.'

'Weak! He's just given us an extraordinary demonstration of sustained strength. Hunter's lucky to have had him for a friend—I hope he'll be as loyal to us.'

'He will, he has no alternative.' And, at his most prim: 'As for his friendship, I'm glad he doesn't like me—at least I know where I stand.'

Both looked at the other four faces as if to seek support

for these differing points of view, but one of the draw-backs of their profession was that they had all been trained not to reveal their thoughts — not even to each other.

4

Catherine Hunter hit the top of her grand piano with the flat of her hand, so hard that all the strings hummed as if in sympathy with her anger. 'But that's . . . that's monstrous, *inhuman!*'

MacAlistair noted that she was using the same word to describe her husband's behaviour as he had used, in his thoughts, regarding his colleagues. Why not? They were one and the same.

'All right, I understand he couldn't warn us before he disappeared. Or do I? Anyway I can accept it. But not to get in touch with me after a whole *week!* Knowing how I'd be feeling! Oh God, *no!*' She moved convulsively from the piano and began to rage around the pretty room. 'No, no, no!'

MacAlistair watched her, wondering about in-humanity. He had just dragged her from one untruth, Alex's drowning, and hurled her savagely into another, the whole ridiculous fable which he had invented for her son on the terrace in Tenerife, and to which he was there-fore committed. Beyond that lay . . . what? Yet more lies, or the painful truth itself? As yet there was no means of telling. A desire for honesty was creeping up on him, something it did every few years. However inhuman his work forced him to be, the sad fact remained that he belonged to the genus *Homo sapiens,* and was subject to all its weaknesses as well as its puny strengths; because he liked Catherine Hunter very much indeed and had never, thank heaven, gone to bed with her, he felt human pity rising inside him like vomit; but he said, truthfully enough, 'He was in terrible danger, don't forget that—maybe he still is.'

She gave him a wild look. For an instant he thought that she hadn't believed one word of the preposterous story and was about to tell him so. But no; as a woman she had accepted, or bypassed, the fragile practicalities of the fable and was affronted by its personal implications. 'So now I'm supposed to rush off to Vienna and hold his hand, tell him I love him, beg him to come home and be a brave boy! Why should I, Patrick, give me one good reason why I should?' Catherine was herself shocked by this reaction to the news. At one moment she had been lying on her bed, moping, actually *aching* with the loss of Alex, and at the next, when she should have been weeping with joy and laughing through the tears, here she was hating him more virulently than ever before—and why the hell not?—when what she had truly thought to be the final, tragic absence now turned out to be the most callous of them all.

'He's deceived me all along—no, don't deny it, I *know*. But this . . . this . . . I won't go, Patrick. If he wants to come back let *him* do the begging.'

MacAlistair could share her rage. Hadn't he once called her husband a high-minded hypocrite with no regard for his responsibilities? Right now, if he allowed himself to do so, he could hate Alex Hunter just as wholeheartedly as she could. Devotion to the selfish bastard had landed them both in impossible situations; his might not be as emotionally shattering as hers—he was in possession of too many hard facts of which she was ignorant—but it was a lot more dangerous.

The blighted human being imprisoned within him admired and respected her refusal to go to Vienna, but the other man, very well, the inhuman one, was going to have to *make* her go, as a matter of self-preservation. Nor would this be very difficult because, as she herself knew in spite of her rage, she loved Alex Hunter and probably always would.

Catherine was rearranging the cushions on the sofa, not thinking about them, hitting them hard: the very sofa on which MacAlistair had once attempted seduction. Already the anger was ebbing, to be replaced by . . . not by relief certainly, how could she be relieved that a man like Alex, so full of malign ambiguities, was threatening to re-enter her life? Surely not by happiness? That would be too absurd! She stood there clutching a cushion, refusing to believe that what she was beginning to feel might indeed be happiness. She remembered now, on the beach at Medano, she had thought that anything would be better than the inert finality of death. Anything? She shook her head, as angry with herself now as with her husband. More weakly, she said, 'For God's sake, he could have let me *know*!'

This was the first thing David heard as he let himself into the flat: his mother's voice saying, 'For God's sake, he could have let me *know*!' He realized at once that she must be talking to MacAlistair who, for his own reasons, devious no doubt, had just told her the very thing which he had been screwing up his courage all afternoon to tell her himself: that Alex Hunter was still alive.

He stood in the hall, clutching *Malnutrition, The Non-Existent Enemy*, hesitant, unsure: of what attitude he would be expected to adopt once he made an appearance: of whether or not MacAlistair had admitted his prior knowledge: of his ability as an actor if called upon to play Ignorance. He had entered very quietly, a strange aspect of his new behaviour which surprised and sometimes revolted him; he would have been unable to say exactly why he had adopted the precaution, but now realized that it was in anticipation of just such an eventuality as this.

MacAlistair was reiterating the well-known reply: Alex Hunter hadn't dared say a word to his family for fear of involving them, submitting them to the very danger from which he was escaping, etcetera. Heard from the wings, as it were, the lines rang less true than ever. David hoped that if he stood very still, MacAlistair, speaking to his mother, might actually mention the missing link omitted when he himself had been told the same story. But this was not to be. It took more than the caution of a nineteen-year-old amateur to deceive the field-man's trained ear. The drawing-room door swung silently open; as the familiar view widened before him David saw that his mother was standing with her back to him staring out of one of the tall windows. MacAlistair gave him a look, half-closed the door, and said, 'Of course I haven't said anything to Davey. Where is he?'

'Out. There was some book he wanted to buy.'

'It'll be a shock. Thank God Anne's gone back to school.'

'I'll have to tell her.' An intensified clarity in his mother's voice informed David that she had turned; he slipped into the dining-room.

'Not just yet, Catherine. Let's be quite sure where we all stand.'

'Perhaps you're right. Why Vienna, Patrick?'

'I don't know, he didn't say on the phone; he was in a hurry, not very coherent, not himself at all.'

The effortless manner in which all this additional information was being passed to him fascinated David, and at the same time struck him as being more than ever suspicious. A man who could hoodwink his mother so convincingly was surely capable of hoodwinking anybody on any subject. As if to reinforce the thought, MacAlistair now said, 'When David comes home I think I'd better break it to him alone, don't you?'

'Yes.' Uncertainly. Then, having thought about it: 'Yes, I do.'

'What time are you expecting him?'

'Any minute.'

'I'll wait.'

David was not all sure that he liked being MacAlistair's fellow conspirator or approved of himself in the part; but he accepted the situation because it was obviously sensible. *Why* was MacAlistair so good at this kind of thing? How did he know that the correct behaviour when somebody was using your beer-glass for target practice was to sit still? It was hardly an everyday occurrence! How did he know that, given the information just relayed, David would now leave the flat as quietly as he had entered it and, after a decent pause, make a noisy return?

He allowed a good ten minutes to pass before acting this out: pounding up the stairs, rattling his latch-key in the lock, entering with innocent face to find MacAlistair framed in the drawing-room doorway, waiting. He gestured, to indicate that the room was now empty; then said loudly and for effect, 'Hi, Davey! Your mother said you'd be back any minute. Come on in, I have something to tell you.'

David went into the drawing-room. MacAlistair shut the door. They regarded each other in silence.

'Did he really phone you from Vienna?'

'Yes.'

'About time! How is he?'

'All right — in the circumstances.'

'What's he doing?'

'Playing it safe, very safe. Can't say I blame him.'

'Is Mother okay?'

'Well . . . it was a shock — you heard. She was angry at first, like you, but she'll get over it.'

'What about his . . . your shady deals?'

'She didn't seem to care about that, you know what women are like.'

David had tuned himself to such a pitch of suspicion, particularly in view of his determination to tell his mother the truth, that the very fact of MacAlistair's having forestalled him struck disturbing resonances. Perhaps he never *would* feel safe or sane again; perhaps he was going to suspect everything of being double for the rest of his life; this might even be what people called 'growing up'. It seemed to him that there was a change in MacAlistair now: something so subtle that he was unable to grasp and analyse it: something more . . . wary, was that the right word? Anyway, MacAlistair wasn't the only one who could play games. He said, 'You know those glasses Father uses for reading?'

At this abrupt change of direction the wariness, if that's what it was, increased suddenly. 'Yes.'

'Were his eyes always bad? I mean, they can't have been bad in the army.'

'No. No, he started using them . . . oh, about ten years ago, you probably can't remember. Why?'

'I just wondered. My eyes have been playing up a bit, I thought it might be hereditary.' How easily the lies slipped off his tongue these days. 'Is his sight very bad?'

'Not very—quite.' The look which MacAlistair was now giving him aroused a memory. Yes, he had directed the same looked at 'Andrew Castle', or whatever he was called, down there on the rocks: deeply searching. 'Castle' had been asking questions too.

David wasn't sure whether his father had been fooling MacAlistair with the false glasses as he had fooled everyone else, or whether MacAlistair knew that they were false and was choosing to be ignorant of the fact; he suspected the latter explanation but was unable to make sense of it.

He was disturbed by the intensity with which the man

was examining him, and so moved away, putting down his book and taking off his coat. How was he to know that this movement was the very thing that MacAlistair was waiting for, the very thing which he himself, under such scrutiny, would never in a thousand years have allowed himself to do, betraying as it did the troubled mind, the uneasy conscience, the questions asked for reasons other than those apparent?

David said, 'Vienna—why Vienna? I mean . . . is there some special reason?'

Special reason! Dear God! Poor kid, poor Catherine, where the hell was all this going to end? 'No. He just thought it was a good place to hide.' Even as he lied, Renata's face arose out of his memory, staring fiercely. Those extraordinary golden eyes—the lioness!

'So? What's the next move?'

'We're going there. You, your mother, me.' He turned away to the window, realizing that the young man, with his new comprehension of things, would probably suspect him for doing so; he didn't care, he was tired, bone-tired of evasions and tricks and a multiplicity of lies. That inquisition in Lorenz's stuffy office had taken its toll; he wanted to lie down in the dark, alone, or get drunk, or both.

If David had been able to see his face he would have been struck, but not enlightened, by the mixture of fatigue, sadness and intolerable comprehension which it revealed. MacAlistair said, 'We're going to Vienna, we're going to see him, talk to him, try to get through to him, before . . .' He broke off, rubbing both hands over his eyes.

'Before what?'

MacAlistair turned to face him again, a frank and open look. 'Before anyone else finds out where he is.' What he meant, but would never have said, was, 'Before it's too late.' But even that reply, though true, was open to many interpretations.

PART THREE

VIENNA

'Ding-dong bell.'

1

They were flying to Vienna, Catherine Hunter, her son, and Patrick MacAlistair. Europe was blanketed in snow: a dirty blanket, creased with roads, railway lines, canals, blotched with yellow-grey stains made by towns. Each of them was silent, contained within their own thoughts, but Catherine had manœuvred MacAlistair into the seat beside her, which could only mean that she intended to speak to him, while David occupied a place three rows in front of them, where MacAlistair would rather have been.

Leaning back, Catherine turned only her face towards him; she spoke quietly: 'When you first told me he was alive . . . I was upset, I didn't really know or care what I said . . .'

'Forget it. *I* have.' He wished that they could all three of them be struck dumb, there was nothing real to be discussed. He had never set out upon an assignment with less enthusiasm nor looked forward to the outcome, whatever grisly form it might take, with more misgiving.

Catherine persisted: 'No, it's important—to me anyway. I meant a lot of what I said, in a way I still do; but when you see Alex . . .'

When I see Alex, MacAlistair thought, the simplest course, saving an infinity of addlepated strategems, soul-

searching, suffering, would be to shoot him dead before
he has time to open his mouth.

'I want him to know, I want you to tell him that I
do . . . need him. Tell him I love him, Patrick.'

'It could be *days* before I see him.'

'Why? You've got that number.'

Oh to live in a world where having a person's telephone
number meant that you would see them! Not, of course,
that he *did* have Alex's telephone number; on the
contrary, he didn't even know if Alex was in Vienna at
all. However, he had told Catherine and David that
during the imaginary telephone conversation Alex had
given him a number; how else could he explain that he
had made contact when, or if ever, he did?

Catherine said, 'You might even see him tonight.' The
optimism in her voice obliged MacAlistair to groan
inwardly. 'And we may not get another chance to talk
about it alone. I want him back, Patrick, however
difficult things are going to be. We can work it out, I
know we can.'

'I'll tell him.'

'That's all I wanted to say.'

MacAlistair closed his eyes. What a ragbag of false
intentions and misconceptions! Catherine, and David to a
lesser degree, believed that they were on their way to
Vienna to rescue Alex Hunter, an unrescuable man.
They believed, finally, because MacAlistair had coaxed
them into it, that Alex had not telephoned them directly
because he didn't want to involve them in the dangers
which were threatening him. They believed that he had
used MacAlistair as an intermediary because MacAlistair,
as his business partner, was already involved anyway.
They hoped that they would persuade him to return with
them to London, face his angry and powerful Italian
associates and convince them that he had never
doublecrossed them nor wished to do so. In their different

ways both mother and son expected the outcome of their
quest, like the outcome of all fairy-tale quests, to be a
happy one.

Anne Hunter, incarcerated in her boarding-school,
MacAlistair's potent masculinity once more eclipsed by
the fascinating and godly Miss Taggart, believed that
they were going to Vienna to knot various loose ends of
Artifax Ltd (and Inc.) left dangling by her father's
sudden death.

As for MacAlistair, eyes closed, willing himself to
stillness, he believed that the many evils lying in wait for
each of them would have to be sufficient unto the days
thereof, one at a time. Among the things which were
certainly, as opposed to possibly, about to happen, he
could foresee a moment of truth when the fairy-tale
would disappear like pantomime scenery, soaring
upwards to reveal the squalid brick and iron of backstage
reality. He wasn't looking forward to this, he wasn't
looking forward to anything the immediate future held
in store.

His most pressing problem was that for the first time in
many years he had no real freedom of movement; he was
used to being answerable to his superiors, not used to
being under their direct command, a position from which
he could not operate as he intended to operate—there
would have to be changes. Of course he didn't expect to
be trusted; even though he had managed to extricate
himself from the inquisition in Lorenz's office, he was still
outstandingly suspect in a world where suspicion was the
norm. Some people might have thought that he and Alex
were an exception to the rule, but he knew otherwise;
there were no exceptions; if there had been, Alex really
would have called him from Vienna.

After MacAlistair had warned him that Joanna, the
executioner, had just arrived in Tenerife, his last words
were, 'I'll be in touch as soon as possible.' Allowing for the

elasticity of 'as soon as possible', the ensuing silence could conceivably have been meaningless, but Alex Hunter wasn't given to meaningless reactions, positive or negative. MacAlistair suspected the silence of meaning that Alex no longer had any practical use for him. He didn't resent this nor feel hurt by it, in spite of the intimacy of their relationship, in spite of it being the only intimate relationship he had ever known, the situation was too extreme for that. The friendship had survived for a very long time, particularly since it contained within itself, right from the beginning, its own destruct-mechanism which, unless MacAlistair was mistaken, had now been fired. If so, there wasn't much time left; he must get in and out before the charge detonated.

Prior to leaving London he had asked whether the daring Kurt Heldmann had supplied any more information regarding Alex's movements in Austria. The fact that Lorenz had said No, as well as his manner of saying it, confirmed MacAlistair's suspicion that Herr Heldmann would never again be informing on his friends and acquaintances; this inclined him, and Lorenz too no doubt, to believe that Alex *was* in Vienna. But for how long?

MacAlistair knew that he had to move quickly and alone; yet Peter Keach and his merry men were already installed in carefully selected positions; they would be at the airport, they would be close behind on the journey into the city, they would be loitering in the lobby of the Hotel Bristol. How then to move quickly and alone? It was only one of the questions for which he was trying to anticipate answers.

At the airport he was reasonably sure that he spotted one of Keach's observers accompanying them through Customs: an ordinary, fresh-faced young Austrian carrying skis over his shoulder, just a little more watchful than anyone else in the crowd. He also caught a glimpse of the black Mercedes which materialized behind them as their taxi swung out on to the main road. But the disastrous extent of his dependence upon others was not properly demonstrated to him until they were passing through the outskirts at Semmering.

A Volkswagen van shot out of a side-turning and drove straight into them. Instinctively, MacAlistair reached for his gun, and then realized that he didn't have one: it was going to be issued to him, by Keach, after his arrival at the hotel. The taxi-driver leapt out into the snowy slush and the inevitable slanging-match began. MacAlistair was by then satisfying himself that Catherine and David Hunter were all right. Of course they were all right, the driver of the van was an expert: impact not too hard but not too gentle: enough noise to collect a small but interested crowd, and enough damage to the taxi to ensure that another, which just happened to be following, empty, would have to stop and take the travellers for the rest of their journey.

At some point during the transfer of luggage and personnel, somebody among the many eager helpers managed to give Catherine Hunter a jab with a hidden needle: so slight that she never noticed it as such. Long before they reached the Bristol she was feeling faint, the shock perhaps . . .

Shock, MacAlistair's arse! He was horrified at the degree to which his normal alertness had been undermined and drugged, as Catherine had been drugged, by these machinations. He must pull himself together, concentrate on the moment, stop trying to plan ahead, at least until he was locked into his own room and able to give his whole mind to the problem.

Sloshing about in the half-melted snow of the Semmeringer Hauptstrasse, paying the taxi-driver, offering his address in case he should be required as a witness, he was aware of a young man taking photographs; it hardly mattered whether he was a real press-photographer or yet another member of the Keach touring company; pictures of the accident would appear in the evening paper, with the news that the beautiful Frau Hunter, a visitor from London, was suffering from shock: to the consternation of her son, David, and old friend-of-the-family Patrick MacAlistair. Alex Hunter in his hiding-place would read the paper; the appropriate warning would have been issued.

MacAlistair was irritated by the whole mountainous subterfuge, which he knew to be unnecessary. And as they drove on through familiar streets towards the centre of the city, the deeper meaning of what had happened at Semmering began to percolate; the warning was not being directed solely at Alex; he, MacAlistair, was being told all over again, as he had been told during the inquisition as well as at his briefing, 'All right, you're nominally in charge of this operation, but however important you think you are, and indeed may at the moment be, you're only a small part of our machine. We accept that you have tricks up your sleeve, but be wary of how you use them, because we too have our tricks. You're one of our creatures and will do as we direct, or other vans will emerge from side-streets and there will be other accidents.'

The point was driven home even more forcibly upon their arrival at the Bristol, so warm, carefully old-fashioned, welcoming. Catherine Hunter had to be supported across the lobby, apologizing like a true Matheson for her weakness and stupidity. Who should be standing at the porter's desk, consulting an Air Austria timetable, but Peter Keach himself. When the management suggested that they should call their excellent doctor, Keach caught MacAlistair's eye and shook his head imperceptibly.

MacAlistair could rely on Catherine to make her own

protestations, saying that all she needed was a cup of tea and an aspirin, perhaps half an hour on her bed. The management, perfectly accustomed to British upper lips—only the stiffer, and richer, ones would wish to stay at their establishment anyway—were quietly solicitous and said that tea would be served as soon as Frau Hunter rang for it. MacAlistair understood that presently a doctor, chosen by Keach, would appear; he did so, a courtly Viennese of the hand-kissing variety, born and bred to duplicity in this capital city of duplicity; he overruled the lady's protestations, saying that shock was not to be trifled with. Catherine, who was by now feeling very groggy indeed, allowed herself to be given an injection and sent to bed. The doctor withdrew to collect his fee.

MacAlistair suspected that the injection was both an antidote to the original drug, powerful and therefore dangerous if left to its own devices, and a sedative. Whatever it was, Frau Hunter's condition was likely to continue unstable, and her husband would immediately be told about it. Whether the ploy was intended to induce anxiety in him or rage, because he could hardly fail to recognize it for what it was, success seemed assured. It certainly induced rage in MacAlistair; latterly he had been involved in such charades only when they were of his own devising, and in this instance he didn't like any of the parts he was being called upon to play. Not only was he worried about Catherine, there was also the problem of David, who no longer took things at their face value: a very different young man from the one MacAlistair had found talking to 'Andrew Castle' on the rocks in Tenerife: that silent entrance into the flat, those concealed questions about his father's reading glasses, clumsily concealed of course, but it was the intention that mattered. He was at the moment properly and genuinely concerned about his mother, but whereas a week ago there would have been concern and nothing else, now there was concern and barely hidden suspicion, it stood out a mile.

MacAlistair badly needed the solitude of his own room. He opened the door to find Peter Keach sitting in a comfortable armchair, waiting for him.

2

MacAlistair's instant reaction was to note that at least the bedroom door had bolts, two strong old-fashioned brass ones, God bless the Bristol!

Keach, now that he had time to examine him, was looking cool and confident, wearing a chunky black sweater and black après-ski trousers tucked into natty black boots; his scarlet shirt made an effective contrast and went well with the white hair, newly washed, and the macho-moustache. He looked, MacAlistair thought, like an actor, possibly a homosexual one: as good a cover as any.

The counterfeit crash and its aftermath were still rankling. 'Well, *that* was a goddam waste of time.'

'I agree.' Keach spread his hands as if to add, We are at the mercy of our masters. At the same time he hardly bothered to hide his smug enjoyment of the situation: he, the put-upon underling, was now in charge and the omnipotent MacAlistair must take orders from him. The Irish, in MacAlistair's opinion, were all the same. He said, 'Do they think he's going to jump out of hiding to sit by her bed?'

'Obviously not, but at least he'll know you're all here.'

MacAlistair moved forward and stood over the younger man, towering. Keach immediately felt at a disadvantage, but that was his fault, he should have stood up as soon as MacAlistair appeared; had not done so in order to demonstrate his ease as a commander, and could not do so now without revealing a sense of inferiority. 'We'd better check the procedure.'

'Not again!'

'Orders.' There was something stilted about his manner which caused MacAlistair's eye to wander casually around the room, seeking likely places for a bugging device. 'We're in your hands of course.'

'You'd better believe it!'

'Nobody's going to move until you give the word. You say you can find Hunter within a few days, no help from us.'

'Correct.'

'You're then going to gain his confidence.'

'I have his confidence—as much as I ever did.'

Keach adopted the tone of a martyr. 'Gain his confidence or consolidate it. You're then going to manoeuvre him into a position where the grab can be made.'

'Correct.'

'With a minimum of force, as quietly as possible.'

MacAlistair nodded absently; he had decided that the bug was either attached to a Biedermeier cabinet with a good deal of fancy brasswork, or it was in one of the electric-light sockets, probably the one by the bed in case he made any subversive telephone calls. 'This minimum of force, does that mean you're operating without Austrian sanction?'

Keach smoothed the moustache and looked affronted. 'The Austrians are co-operating at government level. Not openly, of course.'

'They usually refuse.'

'Ah,' said Keach, 'but Ivan is just over there—' he pointed—'and they don't want trouble with Ivan, do they? That's the number one policy here, same as in Finland. So they're co-operating.' This was no trumped-up excuse; in Russian eyes Alex Hunter *was* trouble, trouble personified.

'As for how you make contact,' still smoothing the moustache, 'nobody's demanding you should use Mrs Hunter and the boy, but if you've got better bait we'll all be interested to see what it is.'

MacAlistair would like to have replied, 'Of course I shan't be using them to make contact, you jumped-up jackass, because I could walk out of this room right now and make the contact within twenty minutes. On my own, without even a magic wand.' But all he said was, 'Whatever the bait, it's not much good sitting by the pond all day when the fish isn't even in it. Or are you that kind of fisherman?'

Keach decided to laugh at this, but there was anger behind his eyes. MacAlistair continued: 'You're not even sure Alex is here.'

'Heldmann said—'

'Ever met Heldmann?'

'No.'

'Take it from me, he couldn't tell the truth if he tried, he'd choke on it.'

'Lorenz may know better.'

This gave MacAlistair the chance to laugh; he made the most of it; then said, 'Do I get a gun? Or if somebody pulls one on me do I say, "A moment please, while I call my friend Mr Keach"?'

Keach produced the gun and ammunition, also a large sum of money for incidental expenses. He did it in a manner designed to impress upon the experienced but maverick field-man, yet again, that he was now part of the great machine, no longer a loner. MacAlistair, weary in any case, was further wearied by this lumpen guile. 'Where's Lorenz staying?'

'He's in London.'

'Really?' He wasn't even sure that he believed it, but

managed to make his tone imply that nobody would be
such a fool as to put Keach in sole command of an
important operation. The answering expression on
Keach's face told him very clearly that there was indeed a
bugging device somewhere in the room. 'And where are
you staying?'

'Just across the road at the Imperial.'

Well, that figured: Hitler's old hangout; hence this
bog-waddler's jackboots, there was a storm-trooper
lurking within Peter Keach, within a great many
Irishmen in spite of the charm and the leprechauns. Why
else had they given the germans all that Irish *Lebensraum*
during World War II, harbour for their spies and for
their submarines? With this in mind, he said, 'Forces all
in position? Machine-guns manned? Tanks at the ready?'

'I think we can give you any support you need,'
ignoring the sarcasm with some difficulty. 'By the way, if
you want a Second, any kind of back-up, you have only to
tell me.'

'I'll tell you this, for the hundredth time: I've got to
work alone.'

'I know, I know.'

'If Alex Hunter gets wind of *any* of your goddam back-
up you've had it, he'll cut and run.'

'Understood. Completely.'

But it hadn't been understood, let alone completely.
Walking up the Kärntner Strasse to buy some Kleenex for
Catherine Hunter, pleased to be in Vienna again in spite
of the circumstances, he realized he was being followed;
realized that the follower was making no effort to conceal
the fact; realized a second later that it was Acton,
'Andrew Castle' himself. Instantly the pleasure of being in
Vienna disappeared: the pretty shop-windows, the ice-dry
nip of the air, the soaring steeple of St Stephen's, snow-
dusted, piercing a snow-soft sky—all consumed by anger.

He turned on Acton who was gazing vacuously at a display of women's underwear. 'For your information, this'll get us both shot.'

Acton shook his head and smiled. 'Nobody will see me, unless I want them to.'

'We're not dealing with cretins.' The owlish eyes behind the glasses didn't deceive him for an instant, the boy was a thug. 'They could be watching us right now.'

Acton glanced at his watch. 'Not yet, the late edition isn't out for another half-hour.'

'David Hunter would recognize you at once, then what?'

'Won't get the chance. And if he does it'll all fit in with your story, won't it? I was after his father in Tenerife, I'm still after him here.'

The logic, but much more the fact that he hadn't foreseen it, chilled MacAlistair. David's trust in him, which might yet prove vital, was precarious enough without Acton upsetting the balance as he had upset it in Tenerife, with disastrous consequences. Lorenz must have had something like this in mind to send him to Vienna at all; most of Peter Keach's private army would be of middle-European extraction, in the interests of camouflage, just as Morales in Tenerife had been Spanish. He said, 'I told them I couldn't operate if I was being followed, you heard me, you were there.'

'Can't have believed you, can they?'

'What are your orders, exactly?'

'That'd be telling.'

'Okay, tell! People make deals, you know—or if you don't it's time you learned.'

Acton considered this, doubtless assessing how much or how little he personally could gain from making such a deal with such a man.

MacAlistair nudged him forward: 'I could be useful to you—what have you got to lose?'

But Acton had made his own decision: 'The same as I lost in Tenerife. Mister Washington was right, you're quite an operator.'

MacAlistair could sense personal animosity in this. He guessed that Lorenz and Amparo had sensed it too, and worked on it; Acton didn't intend to be outwitted again. But his refusal to answer had been an answer in itself: the intention was to follow MacAlistair all the time, everywhere he went.

Having resisted temptation, Acton was now inclined to be cocky: 'I'm pretty good. No one'll know I'm there unless I want them to, only you.'

Yes, he had the nerve all right, and the essential callousness; did he have the brain? Probably not, time would tell. MacAlistair turned away and went into a drugstore; on re-emerging he ignored Acton, who was still taking no pains to conceal himself, and walked slowly back to the hotel.

The Opera was glowing with light prior to the evening performance: *Götterdämmerung* with a superb cast. MacAlistair considered buying a ticket, singles were often available at the last moment if you knew how to go about it; four hours of *Götterdämmerung* would do Acton a world of good! But he knew that he himself was too much on edge to enjoy it, there were too many important problems demanding his attention. In any case, Acton was bound to be the Lead-man; some less important Second would be assigned to Wagner, and he, almost certainly being of German extraction, might even enjoy it. Not at all the point of the operation!

But the carefully rehearsed surprises were not yet over: the crash, the drug, Acton, and now, as MacAlistair turned from the Kärntner Strasse into the Ring, when he was only a few yards from the entrance to the Bristol, a small neat figure came out of the hotel; he didn't actually look towards MacAlistair but paused for a moment, pulling a pair of smart leather gloves on to strong but delicate hands. Immediately MacAlistair experienced the old, well-known feeling in the small of the back; for the man was Joanna, Ernst Weber the executioner who could easily pass for a Viennese and indeed may have been one. He allowed the tall American to get a good view of his profile before he turned it away into growing darkness.

MacAlistair smiled grimly and went into the warm lobby. 'You are being watched,' they had said, 'and if you make any unwise moves you'll get a bullet in your back, courtesy of the man who never misses.' Nice people, but on the whole, he thought to himself as he collected his key, foolish. Again, time would tell.

3

Catherine Hunter had been given a corner suite. Chinoiserie was the motif, nothing delicate, a solid Austrian chinoiserie, altogether endearing. David was standing at the window, watching veils of powdery snow glitter across the street-lamps, when he heard his mother speak from the bedroom: whether to him or to someone in a dream he couldn't tell, she was still half-asleep.

'How do you feel?'

'Oh . . . stupid. Stupid and drowsy.'

David would have liked to ask her a number of practical questions concerning the accident. Even allowing for the eccentricities of Viennese driving, about which he had been told, the absolute lack of caution exhibited by the driver of the Volkswagen van seemed to him to require explanation; the man hadn't been drunk, visibility was perfect, he must have known that he was approaching the main road from the airport . . .

But his mother was in no state to be asked questions;

she smiled at him sleepily. 'I was dreaming, it was a lovely dream.' He sat down on the edge of the bed and she took his hand. 'We were all living in a little wooden house on a mountainside, you and Annie had been ski-ing, snow-balling, I don't know, you were covered in snow. We were all so happy.'

There was something childlike about this which touched her son and made him feel older than she was; for the first time he realized that innocence could be heart-breaking; yet was he himself so much less innocent? His suspicions were all that differentiated them, and they were almost as ephemeral as the dry snow whirling outside the window.

She said, 'We could go away, all of us, would you mind that? Would Annie?' Her voice was soft, the voice of her dream. 'The States—it wouldn't interrupt your studies. Or Canada.' The wooden house on the mountainside was calling her again; her eyelids were heavy. 'Your father could . . . go on with his business there.'

Presently her grip on his hand loosened; she was smiling in her sleep; somewhere on a snowy slope they were all together and happy, and David was left alone with his unasked questions. The impact of the crash had not been great, the taxi had swung away from it because of the slippery road. She hadn't hit her head, she had been thrown on to him, and even he hadn't hit his head; and she wasn't given to fainting, she was a Matheson. The effect was out of all proportion to the cause—hadn't this been the problem since the day of his father's 'death'? Cause and effect in disjunction. He had suspected then; and time had proved him right. He suspected now; what would time prove?

By the time MacAlistair returned with her Kleenex, Catherine Hunter was deep in untroubled sleep. Looking down at her, he felt the old pang of pity; the best of a very bad situation was the sleep itself; after what she'd been

through she probably needed it, and she certainly needed
it before going through what was yet to come!

Looking up, he met her level grey eyes in her son's face.
David was wondering whether to ask him what *he* had
thought of the accident, but something in the older man's
look told him that the answers, if any, would be evasive.
MacAlistair, knowing that the questions were there,
thanked God for small mercies that they were not going to
be asked. He gestured towards the sleeping woman and
said, 'We'd better dine at the hotel.'

'Yes.'

'In about an hour. Okay?' He escaped to the sanctuary
of his own room and bolted the door, shutting himself up
with his plans which, if he were to survive, would have to
be one step ahead of Lorenz, Keach, Acton; always one
step ahead. In the end he didn't even bother to search for
bugging devices. Why bother? They couldn't bug his
thoughts.

The grand-hotel dining-room of the Bristol was almost
empty; it was far too early for the Viennese and, at the
price, there were better and more amusing places. Had it
not been for his mother, David would have liked to
patronize one of them, rather than this mausoleum;
MacAlistair didn't particularly care where he was, his
mind was absent anyway, still occupied with its many
calculations.

His hour of solitude, preceded by the conversation with
Acton and the glimpse of deadly Joanna, had produced
no positive answers to the thicket of questions
surrounding him, but it had consolidated his resolve to
adjust the balance of power to his own advantage: it was
impossible to move in any direction with Acton
immediately behind him.

'Have you spoken to Father yet?'

The question jerked him back to the present, with all

its complex and inessential pretences; but they too had to
be maintained, and David himself must not be underrated. After four hours in the city it would seem
unreasonable if MacAlistair had not tried to use the
imaginary telephone number; so he said, 'Yes.'

'When will we see him?'

When indeed, and under what malign circumstances?
'There's a slight problem here, Davey. He has this idea
that . . . other people in Vienna are looking for him.' If
you must lie, advised the manual, always make the lie as
near to the truth as possible.

David grimaced.

'He's still absolutely determined not to get you or your
mother mixed up in it. He wasn't even very keen to see
me.'

'But he will.'

'Yes, I'm sure he will. The trouble is we don't know
where he is, we have to wait until *he's* good and ready.'

'How did he seem?'

'To tell you the truth, and its only an opinion, I think
the whole thing's become a kind of obsession.' He seemed
to be listening to himself from far away.

'Being hunted?'

'Yes. I told him there's been nothing more from
Andreotti. When we were in London I spoke to
Fairweather — remember Fairweather, the middle man —
and he's heard nothing either. He thinks Andreotti has
discounted the whole deal, severed the connection, set up
other channels.' The further he elaborated the fairy-story
the more intolerable he found it. Why should he, one of
the best damn field-men in the business, who could sell
his services anywhere, yes, *anywhere*, be trapped here in
this cavernous dining-room, spinning yarns to a boy who
only half-believed them?

But careful, careful! Perhaps anger and impatience
were exactly what those others expected of him; by giving

way to them, was he already stumbling into an even deeper trap?

He badly wanted to return to his solitude behind the shining brass bolts. Setting aside the matter of Acton for the moment, he must get his priorities in order, throw away a mass of unimportant debris, store possible contingencies in his mind's computer; then he must sleep, a minimum of six hours, drug-induced if necessary, and tonight it would be necessary; and tomorrow morning he must move, decisively and without hesitation, Acton or no Acton.

'That's it,' he heard himself saying. 'If I can calm him down, get him to see you, let him talk to your mother, I'm sure we can all reassure him, lead him back to a normal way of thinking . . .' Who in God's name was he talking about? Not Alex, that dedicated, incisive man of action who had barely suffered a moment's indecision in his entire life: a man so essentially self-contained that he could accept and rationalize the supreme selfishness: that of marrying a wife and begetting this boy and his sister. 'Calm him down!', 'reassure him!', 'lead him!', what unmitigated crap! Somewhere in this city at this second, Alex Hunter, calm and assured, ever the leader, was deliberately and wisely ignoring the fact that his wife and son were at the Bristol waiting for word of him.

MacAlistair knew most of the love-hate theories and fully recognized the enigma in his own relationship with Alex, but never to his knowledge had the hatred been so intense as it was at this moment, over dinner in the monumental calm of the Bristol's dining-room. Alex had committed an egotistical act of pure folly, never mind the noble motives, and had expected his old friend to help him escape retribution: *expected* it, utterly ignoring the fact that by doing so his old friend became an accomplice, an accessary. And now he was content to sit quietly in some warren in this city of warrens, every one of which was known to him, while his old friend dug himself deeper and deeper into the shit! Trapped, surrounded, and, yes, in danger of being executed. Not to put too fine a point on it, *fuck* Alex Hunter!

But again, careful! The men who had trapped him knew his character as well as Alex did. 'Let him stew,' they must have said, 'he'll play it our way in the end.' Ah, in the end he might, but the end was not yet, not by a long chalk!

'Tomorrow,' he was saying, 'I'm going to ring that number again; get him to meet me, somewhere private, anonymous, wherever he likes. That's the first step . . .' If you must lie, always make the lie as near to the truth as possible.

4

In the operation of following, or trailing, the manual also counselled, it was the business of the Lead-man to keep the Subject in sight; his Second must at all times keep the Lead-man in sight but not necessarily the Subject. Only in an emergency should the Second close with the Lead-man, bearing in mind that by doing so he would be risking his cover and, very possibly, revealing himself to the Subject.

It was a bright clear morning; a heavy frost during the night had solidified any slush which the industrious Viennese had allowed to lie, but otherwise streets and pavements were as dry as if it were midsummer. The icy air stung nose and mouth, titillated the senses, a perfect morning for decisive deeds.

MacAlistair realized that Acton had changed tactics now that Alex Hunter had been warned by the late edition of the evening paper, if not more personally, that

his wife, son, and Patrick MacAlistair were in town.
Perhaps, as he had claimed, he *was* good; it took
MacAlistair a little longer than usual to isolate him from
the crowd, and then only by leading him down streets
which he knew were normally quiet and across some of
the vast open spaces to which Habsburg town-planners
had been addicted. In the Schwarzenbergplatz—speed
circuit for demonic Austrian drivers, dominated by the
appalling Russian war memorial, bane of the city but
tolerated because of Ivan's geographical proxim-
ity—MacAlistair finally identified a leather-coated, fur-
hatted, typically middle-European figure as Acton in
fancy-dress. His Second might have been any one of a
hundred people scattered across the open spaces of the
square. Unfortunately they would both draw closer when
MacAlistair turned into side streets, but that need not be
quite yet; and away to his right, beyond the smaller Karlsplatz, he had spied evidence of what he was looking for, a
construction-site nearing completion: twirling cranes,
jabbering riveters and jack-hammers, all that the heart
could desire.

He strolled towards it, paused to inspect the
Karlskirche which he had always disliked; indeed he
disliked most of Vienna's vaunted imperial architecture,
as heavy and ponderous as the Habsburg monarchy itself.
Acton kept his distance. Let him think . . . What? That
MacAlistair was heading for a secret assignation in one of
the museums. Conventional, but then he had a strong
feeling that Acton was conventional.

The new building was being erected in the Resselgasse,
a small street much too close to MacAlistair's real
destination; but this hardly mattered because if they
knew what the destination was, and he had no positive
proof that they didn't, Keach would be waiting for him
there with gun; and if they didn't know, then the distance
to be covered was conveniently short. A lot depended on

the quality of Acton's Second, but MacAlistair had to risk that; it would be a single throw of the dice, and not the first time that he had gambled on one.

He turned towards the new building, where a railed wooden sidewalk ensured the safety of pedestrians. It was possible that all this was a complete waste of time, but in MacAlistair's experience building operations all over the world were inclined to have certain things in common. Yes, there! A temporary alleyway, taking the place of a tiny street which would be restored once the building was completed. Trucks, machinery of all kinds, had made a mess of the approach, but the night's frost had petrified it into solid ruts and icy puddles. MacAlistair quickened his pace and, just before he reached the alley, broke into a run. Out of the corner of his eye he saw Acton follow suit.

One side of the pavement consisted of rough boards, protecting the site from passers-by and passers-by from the machinery and pitfalls of the site; the ground was treacherously slippery; a woman with a shopping-bag was coming towards him, too intent on picking her way to give him any attention; otherwise the alley was empty. MacAlistair ran past the woman, reached the end of the boarding, swung to his left and into a heavily ornamented doorway which, judging by the row of bells, gave access to a number of old-fashioned flats. If one of the occupants were now to emerge he would be witness to an interesting spectacle. Too bad!

Acton's running footsteps were approaching. As he catapulted into view MacAlistair said, 'Sst! Here!' Acton, by now aware of him in any case, was already slithering to a halt. He turned, regaining his balance, right hand beginning to reappear from the coat pocket. Long before it did so, however, MacAlistair shot him neatly through the forehead, the silenced gun making no sound against the racket of jack-hammer and riveter. Acton, looking surprised (but why?), had still not hit the ground when

MacAlistair dodged past him. He sprinted the remaining ten yards to the end of the alley; in the fraction of a second at his disposal as he hurled himself around the corner, turning right, he was fairly sure that he saw only the back of the woman with the shopping-bag, still picking her way carefully between patches of ice; if there was a running man beyond her he was still some distance away.

MacAlistair now turned left and left again; saw the Wiedner Hauptstrasse directly in front of him. He had doubled back on his tracks, and if any young Second could outmanœuvre him, and have the necessary cool to leave Acton lying where he was, *and* be certain that his instructions permitted him to do so, then he deserved to win the bout and he, MacAlistair, deserved to lose it.

Right into the Hauptstrasse. Stop running, it attracts too much attention in a busy street. Oh God, the terrible vulnerability of one's back, supposing that Joanna was sitting comfortably behind one of those neatly curtained upstairs windows . . . ? Absurd and impossible!

He could see the bookshop on the other side of the road. Traffic-lights were changing, a tram was grinding forward, a certifiable driver was trying to pass it in the face of oncoming traffic: legitimate excuses to run again. He hardly dared look back, but a parked van offered good cover. He turned, peering. No young man was emerging from the side street, but as a precaution MacAlistair kept the van between himself and it as he ran the last few yards and went into the shop.

Nobody was waiting for him with a gun; the cover which Alex Hunter had worked so carefully and so secretly to contrive and maintain was still inviolate after nearly ten years.

Renata recognized him at once. He saw her strange golden eyes flicker over the other three people in the shop. The warning was automatic but irritated him just the same, what did she think he was—a schoolboy? But her instincts had always been infallible, she knew that he badly needed something to shield him from the street; edged him into the space behind a tall bookshelf at the same time asking what she could do for him.

'I'd like to see Herr Stoll.'

'I'm afraid he's not here at the moment. In Munich—the Augstein sale.'

'Of course, I forgot.'

'We should have some interesting things to offer when he returns.'

He thought, what a lioness she is! Tawny and lean, still in beautiful condition. Why had he never found her attractive? Most men did, not that it got them anywhere; she loved Alex and only Alex, from the personal point of view; beyond that she loved all suffering people, all freedoms, all fugitives, all those who shared her hatred with a passion as dangerous as her own. If any single person was responsible for the insane situation in which Alex now found himself it was Renata, but she would never see it that way; it was the rest of the world which was foolish, timid, weak: summit meetings, détente, arms agreements, all pathetic folly! What was needed was action, men worthy of the name, blood, the flames of freedom and revenge rolling across the captive countries, Poland, Hungary, Czechoslovakia, Renata herself upon a white charger, tawny hair flying, leading the raggle-taggle but invincible army of free men, trampling the Kremlin banners into the mud.

The last of the three customers, a student, closed the door upon the two of them; stood on the step for a few seconds gazing at the beautiful edition of Schiller which she had all but given to him: because he was poor and young, and Schiller sang of heroic freedoms. MacAlistair had never known whether to mock or to weep.

She said, 'He saw the piece in the paper, he knows you're here.'

'What did he think of it?'

'I don't know. He loves her, he loves his children.'

'Is that so?'

She despised him for his lack of certainties as much as he despised her for her foolish idealism; they were both brave in the face of danger, and for this she tolerated him and he admired her.

'I must see him.'

She said nothing. He knew that there had been arguments; Alex had convinced her that he was right, 'morally right' in all probability, they believed in those shining clichés which sickened him.

'At once, Renata.'

'Why are you here? Why is she here?'

'Can't you guess, you of all people?'

'They're trying to trap him.'

'Of course, what did you expect?'

The fierce golden eyes searched his face; he was tired of being searched, but bore with it yet again and gave her nothing for her trouble. 'I told him he was a fool if he agreed to meet you.'

'I'm sure you did; you're probably right.'

'Then go away, leave him in peace.'

'Peace!' That really made him laugh, and his laughter angered her. 'He's never been in peace, he never will be, he doesn't want to be.'

'No. He's a fighter, you're not.'

'Right. Fighting bores me, and it's useless.'

With passion, she said, 'Nothing in the world, nothing good or great, has ever been gained without fighting. It should not be so but it is so, because too many men are evil. You know that as well as I do.'

He shook his head; he didn't know it as well as she did. The defiant words were not real to him, but they were real to her and to millions of others, North, South, East, West. And where would it get them, where had it ever got them? Nowhere.

She said, 'Please, Patrick, go away. Take her with you, and the son.'

'Renata, if I could be anywhere else in the world right now, believe me I'd be there. I can't go away, they won't let me, and who's responsible for that?'

'It was the only thing he could do.'

'No it wasn't, he had a dozen options; it was the only thing he *chose* to do. Why can't you people ever accept the results of your actions?'

'We accept all results.'

'Okay, I'm one of them, accept me! I must see him.'

She was deeply troubled, her instincts at war with what Alex had demanded of her. He felt sorry for her; he felt sorry for anybody who had ever had anything to do with Alex Hunter. She shook back the tawny hair and shrugged. She had made her stand, said the things which, so far as she was concerned, had to be said; now she would obey. 'You'll have to wait.'

'I'm alone. Nobody saw me come here.'

'How could that be? If you can't go away, if they won't let you, how could you have come here without them knowing?'

He pulled out his gun and showed it to her. She stared at it, smiled, shook her head.

'All right, look! Go on, look!'

She took it, snapped it open with practised hands; the empty shell flipped on to the floor; she picked it up, felt it, possibly it was still warm. Then she handed the gun back to him, put the shell in her pocket—tell-tale evidence, she knew all about that—and said, 'You'll still have to wait.'

'Okay.'

And so he waited: in the small office behind the shop.

Beyond it there was a dark passageway leading to a
lavatory and a tiny kitchen. In the kitchen was a cleaning
cupboard; the rear wall, brooms, mops and all, swung
back into a small bare cell with an iron bed in it, no
windows. Many beloved fugitives from Budapest,
Cracow, Prague, had thanked God and Renata and Herr
Stoll for this cell, hiding there until identity or plane-
tickets or explosive or whatever it was they needed had
been found for them. If Keach were to appear right now,
MacAlistair himself would slip into the broom cupboard.

Meanwhile he waited. An hour, two hours. Customers
and 'customers' entered and spoke to Renata; among the
latter MacAlistair only recognized one by name, Josef, a
lank dank sallow individual, Czech by birth, who worked
somewhere in the area and had made it his business to
know every inch of it; if anything was new in the whole of
the 4th District, Josef added it to his dossier: new car in
the Belvederegasse — the Stockers had sold their Opel:
furniture van in the Rubensgasse — that young doctor was
moving, going to Linz, the new people were from the 15th
District, needed to be nearer the Opera, he was a second
violin.

MacAlistair knew exactly what was happening. Alex
had guessed, of course, that there was more to the arrival
of his wife, son, and business partner than met the eye;
and he knew that by the very act of assisting him,
MacAlistair had laid himself open to intolerable pressure,
could even be under near-arrest. The 4th District within
half a mile of the bookshop was being methodically
dissected; only when they were satisfied that MacAlistair
was, for the moment at any rate, entirely on his own,
would the next move be made.

He wondered what effect his killing of Acton would
have upon Keach, upon the hierarchy beyond him. God
knows, he'd warned them enough times! It was all very
well not to trust him, but to expect results from him and

then create a situation which ensured that no results could be obtained, that was stupidity. They all worked in a business where momentary carelessness, let alone stupidity, could lead to death. And it had. The reactions would be interesting.

5

'Five-nine-seven-nine.'

'Peter here.'

'Hi, Peter, how's it going? Having a good time?'

'No. The weather's terrible.'

Eddie Amparo looked up sharply at Lorenz. They were sitting on either side of the desk in the office behind the Cavendish Gallery. Lorenz picked up the extension phone. Amparo said, 'What's the matter, snow?'

'Yes, very heavy. Conrad went ski-ing and had an accident.'

'Bad?'

'I'm afraid so—as bad as possible.'

'How did it happen?'

'He collided with Jennings on a steep slope.'

Into the phone, Lorenz said, 'Wait!' He covered the mouthpiece, Amparo did the same. 'Did I understand that correctly? MacAlistair has *killed* Acton.'

'Yes.'

'God in heaven!' Lorenz never swore; the mild expletive fell from his lips like a thunderclap. 'I'll handle this. Hello, Peter?'

'Yes.'

'Where's Jennings now?'

'I don't know.'

Amparo sat back, listening, wedged into his chair, staring at the scarlet and black triangles over the desk.

Lorenz said, 'You don't know! What were all your friends doing?'

'Everything was going fine, we were all having a good time. Then the accident happened, just like that.'

'Nobody witnessed it?'

'No.'

'Mrs Martin and young Martin weren't involved?'

'No. They haven't been told yet.'

'Look after them, we don't want *them* having any accidents.'

'They're fine. Plenty of friends.'

'Good. Where are you now?'

'At my hotel.'

'Wait there until I call you back.'

In Vienna, Keach was sitting on his bed; he put both hands over his face, elbows on knees, an attitude of despair.

In London, Amparo said, 'I should have gone there myself.'

'Easy to say that now.'

'I said it before. Keach isn't big enough for MacAlistair.'

Lorenz gave him a pale glare; then picked up the house-phone; his receptionist answered. 'Mary, get on to Transport — I want to go to Vienna immediately.'

Amparo heaved himself out of the chair and began to prowl about the office with the light tread commanded by some very heavy men. 'What'll you do with Keach?'

'Take over. Make sure he isn't caught again with his pants down.'

'He'd better be replaced.'

'We'll see. You can't really judge a man because MacAlistair gets the better of him.'

'That bastard! He's gone to see Hunter, of course.'

'Of course.'

6

MacAlistair was still waiting. Four hours, five hours. By God, they must be taking the whole of the 4th District apart, brick by brick!

He wondered whether the hand-kissing doctor had again called to see Catherine Hunter or whether she was now going to be allowed to recover. There was nothing he could have done about this, he decided; it was their ploy, they might or might not be aiming with it at something beyond his line of sight; he was inclined to think not, it had been merely an attention-getting device, a clumsy one.

During these hours of waiting, Renata brought him excellent coffee and open sandwiches from the café across the street, but otherwise made a point of being busy in the shop and thus unable to talk; she had had her say, and that was that; she never indulged in idle conversation and she detested gossip: unusual in a Hungarian: or was she a Czech? He had never known, perhaps she didn't know herself. During the terrrible years of war and occupation her mother had been raped by a foreign soldier. A Russian? The lioness had been conceived in violence and rage, it was in her blood.

Long ago, when 'Operation Resistance' was first instigated, she was considered perfect recruitment material: fierce, loyal, hating; and there were thousands like her, half middle-Europe, it must have seemed in those days. Things changed, for the worse she would always claim; the fire and the passion were intentionally cooled into more purposeful action; even the too explicit name was changed to 'Group R'. It became necessary to establish an Austrian headquarters; Alex was given the job.

He at once appreciated that there must be two headquarters, the first an official one, known to the Officials, the second a secret one, known for what it really was to only a few; and the two must be kept totally apart from each other, the job was as dangerous as that. So the bookshop had come into being; so Renata, no longer a young firebrand, had disappeared from the ranks of the soldiers, had reappeared as Frau Stoll; her husband spent much of his time away on business; it was understood that they operated another shop in Amsterdam, had connections in Paris and London. Herr Stoll was not often in Vienna, but that didn't stop Renata loving him — any more than his absences from London had stopped Catherine Hunter loving him.

Six hours.

Renata came into the office and said, 'You really did kill a man.'

'I told you I did.'

She smiled grimly. 'We can go now. This way.'

At the side of the shop was a door giving into one of those vast entrance gateways common to most European cities. There had been a great mansion here once. The entrance ran through the thickness of the street-facing houses before emerging into what had been a fine inner courtyard. The centre of it was now occupied by a low building in which worked a chair-mender, a welder, and a willowy girl who made sturdy but ugly pots. These artisans, as well as the people who lived in various apartments burrowed out of the once-great house, used another entrance leading into a side-street. The tunnel next to the bookshop was roughly boarded off from the courtyard, serving as a garage for the delivery van and for Renata's Simca.

MacAlistair lay down on the floor in the back of the latter; Renata placed a rug over him and threw her shopping basket, some old newspapers and an overcoat on top of it. Josef opened the gate and she drove out into the Wiedner Hauptstrasse.

He wasn't really interested in where they were going, but so ingrained were the field-man's habits that automatically, without thinking, he found himself visualizing their journey: downhill — which meant back to the Karlsplatz: and right — which meant roughly north-eastwards: halt at traffic-lights, and then a racing start — across the Schwarzenberg-platz, where else? Did she give Russia's heroic monument the finger? Probably. Onwards, and a lot of traffic — to the right of the Stadtpark, past the Hilton: toot-toot of a barge — the Danube Canal: hollow reverberation — a bridge. Now a number of turns which confused him, but it didn't matter; Alex Hunter was hiding out in the 2nd District somewhere between the Prater and the curve of the canal.

The car stopped. Renata got out and opened the back door slightly; he knew that she was looking up and down the street, perhaps waiting for somebody to pass; then she said, 'Okay, clear.'

He unrolled himself and slid on to the back seat, at the same time bending as if to pick something from the floor, but he needn't have bothered with this subterfuge, there was nobody about. The Simca was parked between blank walls under spindly trees in a typically drab street. Light snow was falling again. He followed her through a gateway into a concrete yard, in at the door which she unlocked and up to the third floor of a depressing apartment-house which dated from the very worst of the post-World War II days when there hadn't been enough money to construct anything properly. And so into the pokey flat where Alex was waiting for him.

The periodical metamorphosis of Alex Hunter into Gustav Stoll had been part of MacAlistair's life for many years, and he had long since ceased to be surprised by it, in some ways he hardly noticed it at all; but of late, and particularly on this January afternoon, he found himself wondering whether perhaps Herr Stoll was not the real man and Mr Hunter the disguise, or, worse still, that both were disguises and the real man was somebody he had never even met.

Stoll was younger than Hunter; he had fair hair as opposed to Hunter's brown, cut short at the sides so that the face, particularly the nose, seemed longer; this hair revealed a noble forehead which was lacking in Hunter, obscured by that lock which he was forever pushing aside. The eyes were sharper because of the contrasting hair, and without the false glasses which softened them. He looked fit and tanned, from Tenerife in fact but why not from ski-ing, taut and handsome. MacAlistair was disturbed to realize that today his first reaction on meeting Herr Stoll was one of impatient irritation; he quelled it.

After their usual offhand greeting, after Renata had brought them a bottle of wine, a plate of wurst, two glasses, after she had retired, Alex Hunter said, 'How's Catherine — Davey?'

'Longing to see you.' Hunter grimaced at the light sarcasm but took no offence to it. 'Pretty unwieldy kind of a trap!'

'God, yes! Forward patrols, artillery, armour in reserve, you name it!'

Hunter shook his head. 'Did you really shoot one of them?'

'Toughie called Acton. Nothing between the eyes — except the bullet.'

'You're in trouble, Mac.'

'No, *you're* in trouble. What are you doing hanging around here anyway?'

'I should have been leaving tomorrow, but . . .' He leaned forward, putting his cheeks in his hands, elbows on knees, a characteristic and boyish pose. 'I want to see them before I go, Catherine and the boy.'

'Don't!'

They regarded each other across the years of their friendship. MacAlistair wondered if he himself seemed as far away as Alex did.

'I must.'

'You just said it—it's a trap.'

'Trap-schnap! We can tie them in knots, they won't even know what hit them.'

'All I can say is: Don't.' He knew that it would have no effect, but imagined that in the years to come he would be able to look back with a certain amount of pride at this moment when he had told the absolute truth, given the most honest advice. If Renata were in the room she would agree with passionate conviction, but this was one of the reasons why she wasn't in the room.

'Mac, I owe it to them.'

'That's debatable.'

'I owe it to myself.'

MacAlistair nodded. Alex had always possessed a very clear idea of what he owed to himself; in most men this would have been selfishness, but not in Alex Hunter; better if it *had* been selfishness.

'I can't just disappear and leave them in mid-air, wondering. I want them to know, I want *her* to know, it's important for all of us.'

'Know?' There were so many things to be known.

'What I am, what I've been doing all these years.'

'Ignorance is safer.'

'No, no! I can't have her thinking I'm some petty little salesman, don't you see?'

'Oh yes, I see.'

'All those phoney business trips. She used to think I was living it up on an expense-account in half the fleshpots of the world, sleeping with anything that took my fancy. I

can't go until I've told her I was . . . something bigger
than that, doing a job that really mattered.'
'Making the world a better place to live in.'
'Yes, and sod your sarcasm!'
MacAlistair shook his head in wonderment.
'Mac, you *know* I've got to do this, you've hit me over
the head with it enough times.'
'I guess we're past that argument now.' Even as he said
it he new that Alex Hunter, being Alex Hunter, would
never be past that argument. As if to prove it, his old
friend said, 'I've played it as straight as I could. Okay, it
caught up with me, you said it would and it has. But I've
got to *end* it as straight as I can.'
'Alex, spare me the moral crap!'
'Mac, spare me the tough cop — that isn't what you are,
and you know I'm right.'
'I know you've never been right, never since the day you
married her, never since you sired those kids. Forget it,
we've played this scene. What do you mean, you're
leaving? Hungary?'
'Czechoslovakia first.'
'That's one of the things they're afraid of. Renata too?'
'No, she's staying here.' He sat back, ran his hands
through the short fair hair; stood up and began to pace.
'That's where I belong, that's where I'm needed.'
'And that's where you'll get yours between the eyes.'
'No.'
'Or a trip to the Gulag.'
'No.' He was excited. MacAlistair witnessed the
excitement with a sinking heart. 'For God's sake, Mac, it's
the logical conclusion, I've been in training for ten years,
I've been training *them* for ten years, and it's all been
leading to this moment. I'm going to *become* them.' His
eyes were alight with certainty. The heroic words came
pat because they had been said before, to Renata.
What had she thought, strong woman, on learning that

the Jekyll and Hyde in this man she loved were about to become one, and lost to her forever? Well, she had encouraged them both, Jekyll the astute political planner, Hyde the crusader with a flaming sword. He was in full spate now: 'They need me, those men and women, they really *need* me. It's a wonderful feeling, Mac, wonderful things will come of it, you'll see. I have more real friends in Hungary, Czechoslovakia, Poland, than I have in the whole of the rest of the world.'

'And another wife?'

That did it! A pin to the balloon of high-minded rhetoric. Alex Hunter turned on him in the cold contemptuous rage which he had witnessed only once before. 'Jesus Christ! You're *nothing*, you're *hollow*!'

'We're both hollow. At least I haven't filled the cavity with crap!'

The other man came nearer, staring at him with hatred, and he regarded it unmoved. He felt that they were particles of some cosmic explosion, flying apart in space at unimaginable speed, disintegrating as they flew. Keeping his voice low out of long habit, and it was no less violent for that, Alex Hunter hissed, 'You filled the cavity with *ice*. God in heaven, what makes you tick?, have you never been *involved*?'

'Never. Basic training.'

'Basic training be buggered! We're dealing with men, women, souls . . .'

'Renata's really got to you, hasn't she?'

'You talk like the bloody hick American you are.'

' "My country 'tis of thee." ' He wondered whether this time Alex was going to hit him, he rather hoped so, for then and only then could he hit the bastard back.

'I'll tell you this, MacAlistair, until Americans *become* involved, they're nothing. All the gold in Fort Knox isn't worth one involved individual.'

'And I'll tell you this, Hunter—you're a selfish sonofabitch!'

'*I'm* selfish!'

'Yes, but that doesn't matter. What makes you so fucking *dangerous* is that you're selfish in the name of others. You're a menace, Alex, you destroy!'

'The way I destroyed Jan Veretka.'

'Oh no, *he's* an ideal, ideals are okay. The way you destroyed your family, the way you're destroying me right now.' He saw something slink away behind the fanatical brown eyes, the eyes which had disturbed him in the photograph on Catherine's dressing-table: it had even accompanied her to Vienna. There was another man imprisoned behind the eyes, an ordinary lovable man who had been banished with the passing of time to ever stronger and more impregnable dungeons, until now there was no escape from him, ever. Rage withdrew like a wave, leaving them both stranded and gasping. Time and again over the years they had been forced, one or the other of them, to make this stand, redefine the vast differences between them.

After a long pause, Hunter said, 'I never meant to hurt my family, you know that.'

'Forget it, I'm sorry I said it!'

'And I'm not destroying you. I asked you to help me, you agreed of your own free will, if you didn't want to . . .'

'Oh God, Alex, of course I want to.' Desperately changing the subject, desperately needing to feel terra firma under his feet again, he added, 'How come you allowed that fink Heldmann to recognize you?'

'That was stupid, I was in a hurry . . .'

'Never hurry. Basic training.'

This time his friend smiled. 'It was the first time, the very first time ever, that I didn't switch identities in Paris—and I walk slap into Heldmann at the airport.'

'Alexander P. Hunter himself—that must have shocked him.'

'It did.'

'Obviously he was coming not going.'

'Yes, thank God! Back from one his erotic trips to Hamburg. I caught up with him the same evening, waited outside his favourite clip-joint on the Annagasse. By that time I was Herr Stoll, and as God's my judge he didn't know me from Adam; mind you, he was pissed.'

'Did they find his body?'

'No. Josef and Rudi were in the taxi, we added him to the rest of the pollution in the Beautiful Blue Danube.'

'So when do you plan to move?'

Alex Hunter came back and sat down opposite him again. 'As soon as I've seen Catherine and Davey.'

MacAlistair sighed deeply. 'Will you never listen to me? Don't see them.'

'How are you going to rig it for me, Mac? Do they really have an army out there?'

'More than twenty men, I don't know how *many* more, I'm persona definitely non grata—thanks to you, you dumb ox!'

They stared at each other for a moment in silence, as if each of them could not quite understand the fury which had possessed them a few minutes before. Alex Hunter shook his head. 'Don't think I won't miss you, I'll miss you a hell of a lot.'

MacAlistair shrugged. 'It isn't the end, we'll probably meet again. In the Treblinka.'

'Probably. Minus our balls. How do we fix it, Mac? What story did you tell Catherine, what on earth does she think I'm doing here?'

This time the fairy-tale seemed even more absurd. Hunter listened to it in silence, dumbfounded. At the end he said, 'They believed *that*?'

'Davey doesn't, not altogether.'

'I should hope not. *My* son.'

'Catherine . . .' MacAlistair could feel the ice bending under his weight, it was very thin. 'She's been . . . conditioned to believe things, hasn't she?' He said it as gently as possible, and Hunter accepted it; but nothing, it seemed, would ever make him accept the total immorality of what he, the moral man, had done. Well—there had been holy fools, he was presumably a holy blind-man. In his blindness he now said again, 'How can we fix it?'

'They don't trust me an inch. I have no freedom of movement, that's why I had to kill the boy.'

'And you made it.'

'The second time won't be so easy.'

'You can't be sure. You may have proved a point.'

'I doubt it.'

'Remember those cafés we used to use over by the Elisabeth-Platz, Argentinierstrasse. Maybe the Sud-bahnhof itself.'

'The station's too open. One of the café's might work.'

'And Keach?'

'Oh, I'd give him the old phoney stake-out; tell him you're meeting somewhere else right the other side of town.'

'Would he fall for that?'

'God knows what he'd fall for. They may be waiting for me at the hotel with a machine-gun.'

Alex Hunter shook his head. 'You're too valuable, Mac.'

'For the moment.'

'For ever. I'm your life-insurance, if you play it right. Who else has a hope of getting anywhere near me? Nobody, and they know it.'

MacAlistair glanced at his watch and stood up. 'Right now I'm pushing my luck—what's left of it! Here's how we move: I go back and see what's cooking, then I do the double-think, then I tell you a time and place.'

'Tomorrow.'

'I hope so. A lot depends on whether Catherine's been allowed to get over her shock.'

'Dumb bloody gambit!'

'Sure was. How do I get word to you? Josef?'

'Why not? The newspaper gag, Herr Muller's.'

MacAlistair considered this; then nodded. 'Herr Muller's, nine o'clock this evening. Tell Josef to ask for . . . *France-Soir*.'

Renata showed him out; she made it quite clear that she would have preferred to stick a knife in his back. There was no need for any security precautions now; nobody had followed them to this out-of-the-way spot, moreover it was dark, and a dusty snow was still falling. He walked to the Praterstern and boarded a tram. Taxi-drivers could always be questioned.

7

There was nobody waiting for MacAlistair in the lobby of the Bristol, as far as he could tell. He collected his key and asked after Frau Hunter, receiving a flood of *gemütlich* by way of reply: she was looking so well today, so lovely, so elegant; she had gone out with her son to see something of their beautiful Vienna, she would perhaps be tempted to do a little shopping. MacAlistair expressed delight at her recovery, heartfelt in view of what she was going to be called upon to do on the morrow. He guessed that Keach would be sitting in his room as before, and was sincerely interested to know how they were now going to play it.

The first thing he saw on opening the door was Lorenz, looking as pale, scrawny, dangerous as ever. Keach, diminished, was standing by the window.

MacAlistair said, 'Well, what an honour!' It didn't matter whether Lorenz had been in Vienna all the time, in spite of what Keach had said, or whether he had just come winging in from London. Here he was, doing his trick with the neck, and saying, 'I don't know what action Washington will order me to take. He was a good man.'

'He was a dummy, or he'd be here now. I told you in London, twice, that I wouldn't get *near* Alex with anyone breathing down my neck. Did you listen? Did you hell!'

'You think that entitles you to kill one of your colleagues?'

'Moreover, Willingdon was there when I said it.'

'I'd adopt another attitude if I were you.'

'If you were me,' said MacAlistair savagely, 'you'd have given me a free hand from the word Go, you'd have had the mother-wit to realize it was your only chance.'

'Acton was . . .'

'Oh, for Christ's sake, let's forget Acton, he's dead. The point of the operation is to find Alex Hunter, right?'

'Of course, but not at the expense . . .'

'Well, I've found him. So let's report *that* to Washington. Right away.'

Lorenz stretched and resettled his neck again. Keach was trying to look efficient and ruthless while at the same time pretending that he wasn't in the room, wasn't listening to any of this sacrilegious insubordination. MacAlistair noticed that he was also more soberly dressed; Lorenz wouldn't have approved of the black and scarlet outfit.

'You've found him?'

'Yes.'

'Where is he?'

'I'm not saying. Anyway, you wouldn't get within a mile of him.' He seemed unable to contain his anger and contempt, perhaps because he'd been bottling them up for too long; this incontinence surprised but didn't alarm

him. Oh God, how preposterous they all were! Yes, all:
not only this pseudo-spymaster who couldn't even buy the
right size in shirts, but equally that one hundred per cent
genuine idealist squatting in a crummy flat in the 2nd
District with one of his wives.

He watched Lorenz trying to digest the news of his
success without recourse to the Hunter family or to the
army which was occupying Vienna under Keach's
command; it was a tough morsel, and it was followed by
another, just as indigestible: the fact that MacAlistair
refused to reveal Alex Hunter's whereabouts. This he was
evidently unable to chew. 'Whether we make any move or
not is up to me. You will certainly tell me where Hunter is
hiding.'

'I will certainly not. If you're capable of putting a half-
witted beginner on my heels, thereby screwing up everything I planned to do, you're perfectly capable of
throwing a cordon around Hunter's hide-out and scaring
him to Timbuctoo.'

'I've no intention of doing anything so stupid.'

'So you say, but you said you wouldn't have me
followed.'

Lorenz thought about this for a time. 'You can bring
him in?'

'Yes. You'll have your sticky paws on him by this time
tomorrow. But it'll be done my way, or no deal.'

'MacAlistair, you're not in a position to make *deals*.'

'I'm not? Then we have nothing to talk about.'

Again Lorenz regarded him in silence, the pale blue
eyes betraying only a mild distaste. Keach was staring at
the wall on the far side of the room like a guardsman on
parade.

MacAlistair knew that he was prone to exaggerate
Lorenz's failings; he was for instance a scrupulously fair
man, no mean attribute considering the position he held,
and he would report MacAlistair's success and his own

miscalculations with equal honesty. No doubt he was now regretting the fact that he had allowed Keach to be present at this interview, but Keach was there and would thus have to witness the face-losing spectacle of Lorenz climbing down. 'Very well, in the circumstances I accept that the operation must be conducted your way. What are you planning to do?'

'Alex wants to see his wife and son.'

'As I thought.'

'No. You thought that they could be used to lure him out.' He glanced at Keach. ' "Bait" was the official term, I believe. What I'm saying is entirely different: *Alex* wants to see *them*, the fact that they happen to be in Vienna is incidental. If they were in London he'd go there.'

Lorenz looked as though he had just bitten into a sour lemon. 'In spite of the fact that he knows they're a trap?'

'Yes. I admitted that, naturally.'

Lorenz could accept this more easily, 'I see. Well, you're known to be an expert juggler, I hope you haven't got too many balls in the air at the same time.'

'Oh, I have, I have.'

Both of them, and perhaps even Keach too, unless he had really turned to the stone he resembled, knew that they were approaching the crux of the matter; and they knew how awkward that crux was going to be, Lorenz with antipathy, MacAlistair with some pleasure: for it was based on a premise in which none of them believed, upon a word which didn't even exist in their vocabulary: trust.

Evidently Lorenz intended to let MacAlistair explain his plan, even though he must have guessed what it was; perhaps that innate honesty forbade him to use the non-existent word. 'What else did you tell Hunter?'

'I said I intended to doublecross you. I said I'd set up the meeting at one place, and at the same time make sure that Keach and his men were staking out another on the opposite side of Vienna.'

'He believed you?'

'Of course. He's an honourable man, I'm his best friend.'

Even Keach's eyes had flicked towards him. Both of them were regarding him with a suspicion so intense that it was almost tangible. MacAlistair returned their look with something remarkably akin to merriment. Lorenz might find it distasteful that the whole plan was based upon unmentionables, he found it enjoyably ironical.

'And where did you arrange to set up this meeting?'

'At a café we both know, in the 4th District, near the Elizabeth-Platz.'

'I see.'

MacAlistair wondered what he saw. Not the truth certainly. But he must control this heady sensation of superiority; Lorenz was a clever man and as sly as they made them. Superiority comes before a fall.

'So you're asking me to believe that you're going to betray your old friend, your close colleague for more than twenty years.'

'Yes, sir.'

Lorenz gave him the anaemic basilisk stare.

'For God's sake, what else can I do? I told you — Alex and I agreed long ago that a situation could arise, on either side, where friendship didn't mean a thing any more. This has to be it.'

Lorenz nodded but said nothing. Keach was still watching him as if prepared to jump should MacAlistair spring in his direction.

'You surely don't think I value his life more than my own: that I'd *really* put Keach up to a phoney stake-out.'

'I think,' said Lorenz with some difficulty, 'that you're quite capable of it.'

Ambiguity had settled on the room like a thick fog;

they could barely see each other through its writhing vapour.

'I also think that we shall have to watch you very carefully indeed to make sure that you don't.'

'You watch me carefully, and I'm not moving an inch.'

Lorenz sighed and looked at his fingernails. It was he, after all, who found himself forced to use the non-existent word: 'If Alex Hunter trusts you, as you say he does, that means you've been helping him all along. He *did* tell you what he'd done, you *did* warn him that we were sending Joanna to Tenerife, though God knows how you found out . . .' He paused, perhaps hoping for elucidation now that they were apparently in partnership again.

MacAlistair said, 'It'll all be in my memoirs.'

'You *did* identify somebody else's body intending to mislead us, not to cover for us as you claimed. That being so, you can't possibly expect us to trust you too.'

'I don't expect it,' said MacAlistair, 'but if you have an option I sure as hell don't know what it is.'

Downstairs in the lobby, he first ascertained that Frau Hunter and her son had returned from their outing; then he went to the hotel bookstall, bought a copy of the evening's *France-Soir*, took it to a writing-desk and wrote to Alex Hunter, as promised: 'The bookshop. Three-thirty tomorrow afternoon.' He slipped the note into *France-Soir*, making sure that a fold would keep it securely in place; then he walked across the Ring to Herr Muller's news kiosk and passed him the paper under cover of buying three others. Herr Muller had proved his loyalty on many occasions; he was a Czech, his name wasn't Muller, and he knew his countryman, Josef, well.

MacAlistair walked back to the hotel, called Catherine Hunter on the house-phone and went up to the suite. Mother and son were waiting for him, as expectant as children on Christmas Eve. If he had needed proof of the kind of man he was, and he didn't, not any more, the equanimity with which he met this childish expectation would have given it to him.

'Yes,' he said, 'I've seen him, he sends you both his love, he's going to play it our way.'

Catherine ran to him, hugged him, kissed his cheek. In the ancient story, he recalled, it was he who should have done the kissing. 'Oh, Patrick, how wonderful! Will he . . . ? Do you think he'll come back with us? Home?'

Home! It wasn't his business to explain that the word had no more meaning for Alex Hunter than it had for him; the difference was that Alex had created a 'home' with the requisite figures to populate it, whereas he had not. Let them all do their own explaining, get on with their own suffering, it was none of his business.

David said, 'When can we see him?'

'Tomorrow afternoon.' And, forestalling more questions: 'I told you, he's playing it safe — it doesn't matter, the only thing that matters is you're going to meet. Right?'

'Where?'

MacAlistair was glad that there were only a few more hours to go; the boy was learning as fast as a baby bird on its first day out of the nest. By this time tomorrow he would either be fully grown or demolished, or both. 'I'll tell you tomorrow, it's better you shouldn't know until the last moment.' And, turning quickly to Catherine: 'You're better, you look great.'

They had spent a fascinating afternoon, walked up to the Belvedere; the lovely formal gardens reminded her of the Luxembourg, but the slope made it more effective — and the pictures! Why had nobody told her about Schiele? Why wasn't he as famous as . . . as Degas? That clarity, that merciless observation, particularly of himself — how fuddy-duddy most of the Impressionists seemed by comparison!

MacAlistair thought, 'Alex was right, I am hollow, a nothing, or I couldn't bear to stand here and watch her face, so full of hopes.' To escape, to escape by embracing them more closely, he took them out to dinner, the Drei Husaren, still one of Europe's better restaurants: soothing piano music, chandeliers, the well-to-do tourist's Vienna; then to a Hungarian place, the kind of place which reduced Renata to a seething fury, where there were violins and cymbalons, the well-to-do tourist's Viennese Hungary.

Wine increased Catherine Hunter's optimism — there was going to be a new life for all of them; wine softened David's suspicions, though occasionally MacAlistair found the grey eyes fixed on him in a kind of puzzlement. By this time, excellent food and maddening music equally disregarded, he had formulated his plan. He tipped the wailing violins and waved them away; then said, 'What were you proposing to do tomorrow, apart from just waiting?'

'We thought . . .' But she dismissed old plans impatiently. 'It doesn't matter now.'

'On the contrary, it matters very much.'

'We thought we'd go to the Riding School; that nice porter's getting us tickets.'

'Good! Go to the Riding School.'

'But oughtn't we to be . . . ready in case Alex changes his mind about the time?'

'He won't.'

David said, 'Why don't you come too?' In this, MacAlistair recognized a widening of suspicion which he would have felt himself: without knowing quite why, the boy wanted to keep him in sight.

'No. I have other things to do.' Many other things, like pulling the wool over half the eyes in Vienna. 'And listen — after the Riding School why not take a look at the Hofburg, the palace? Then you could go to Demels for lunch, it's quite near . . .' He began to explain the age-old argument: whether Demels did or didn't make a better Sachertorte than the Sacher itself, Vienna had always been divided. 'I'll pick you up at Demels at three-fifteen — three-fifteen exactly.'

They were staring at him, frowning. Was he betraying the tension he felt? He didn't know and he no longer cared, the danger was too great, too imminent. He said, 'But there's one thing you must promise me, it's very, very important: once you've left the Bristol to go to the Riding School you mustn't go back there, not on any account.'

David was still watching him intently. *Everybody* was watching him intently, what the hell! 'Why not?'

'Because it's just possible that your father's right, there may be other people in Vienna looking for him. If so, you don't want to lead them straight to him, do you?'

David shook his head, but there was no trust in his eyes.

'Have we got that straight? I'll pick you up at Demels in the Kohlmarkt at three-fifteen exactly and take you to the meeting-place.

Catherine put her hand over his and squeezed it gratefully. 'Don't worry, we'll be there.'

So it was arranged; but when at long last, they all went to bed, MacAlistair was unable to sleep, weary though he was after that endless day which had started with the killing of a man and progressed through a plethora of lies and deeply buried truths to end in the wailing of violins and the tintinnabulation of cymbalons. He had always been unable to sleep when things were either beginning or ending, so now, when things were both beginning *and* ending, what else could he expect? He knocked himself out with blessed drugs. And slept.

8

The day dawned clear, cold, brilliant. The rimed trees outside the hotel sparkled in hard sunshine, the sky was a piercing summer blue. But while Catherine and her son were watching the Lipizzaners, and while MacAlistair was arranging the details of the meeting, clouds appeared in the east, white as distant ski-slopes to begin with, then rising up ponderously to show their snow-bloated bellies, an ominous yellow-grey. By noon the brilliant day had fled away towards Salzburg, and by three o'clock the first hesitant snowflakes were twirling down: not the dusty powder of the days before, but fat white petals which lay for a while on the frozen ground, then faded: then lay more thickly and did not fade.

At three-fifteen precisely MacAlistair entered the crowded turn-of-the-century café in the Kohlmarkt, loud with chatter, fat with cakes. Catherine and David were waiting for him. She was wearing a handsome fur hat to match the collar and cuffs of her coat; her face was shining with expectation. He led them up the street and round the corner to Am Hof where he had left the BMW rented that morning. They set off in the opposite direction to their destination, not in order to confuse anybody who might be following but in compliance with the mysteries of the city's one-way system.

They were silent; the atmosphere in the car was charged with expectancy and emotion, but MacAlistair was insulated against it. As he turned into the Ring and wended his way towards the Wiedner Hauptstrasse yet again, he was dissociating himself expertly from what was happening, from what was about to happen; many years ago he had cast off the shackles of family which bound

these people together so cruelly; what they made of their
predicament was entirely their own business. He checked
the practicalities: by now, Keach and his secret army
would be tucked away on the other side of the city,
glancing at their watches, wondering: by now Alex
Hunter should be on his way from the dismal flat in the
2nd District, huddled on the floor of Renata's Simca
under a clutter of coats and books and baskets.

He parked the car not too far from the shop. As they
walked towards it, he glanced at Catherine's face: brave,
determined, prepared. The snow had not yet made up its
mind whether to enshroud Vienna or to travel a little
further and decorate the mountains. The bookshop was
closed; a handwritten notice informed, 'Open 8 a.m.
tomorrow morning, Wednesday.' Josef unlocked the door
and admitted them, saying to MacAlistair, 'He's not here
yet.' MacAlistair knew that Josef's minions were once
again posted all over the area, watching, guarding.

Catherine and David entered cautiously, silenced by
the significance of the approaching moment, the strange
secrecy of this musty setting. MacAlistair took them
through to the office which was warm, too warm. He had
just forced the window open to admit a little air, Renata
would close it again, when he heard the clang of the yard
gate, the sound of the Simca's arrival. He looked at
mother and son, and made a point of seeing them as
pieces of a puzzle, not as human beings at all. Catherine
was taking off her fur hat and her coat, placing them
carefully on a dilapidated bentwood chair; in this shabby
room which knew so many desperate secrets, they looked
luxurious and strange, objects from another world.

Then the door opened and Alex Hunter came in, or
rather Herr Gustav Stoll came in, followed by Renata and
Josef. Catherine and David recognized him at once, and
at the same time didn't recognize him. MacAlistair,
observing, saw her eyes flick from the tall fair-haired man

who was and was not her husband to the fine, fierce woman accompanying him. Hunter came forward quickly and embraced her, holding her tightly. David stared at Renata, frowning; Renata returned the stare with interest, openly.

MacAlistair said, 'I'm going back to the car, just in case.' And to Josef, 'It's a silver BMW.'

'I know, I saw it.'

'You'll be watching.'

Josef nodded; he was always watching.

'If I see anything at all suspicious I'll switch on the side-lights.' He turned and looked back at Alex Hunter. 'You've got forty-five minutes before Keach could even begin to suspect he's been taken.'

'Thanks, Mac.'

'Let's make it a deadline at four-twenty, to be on the safe side.'

'Okay, four-twenty.' They were used to working to the exact second.

Renata left the office with MacAlistair, closing the door behind her; the Hunters could be seen through its glass panels, abandoned to their privacy. She said, 'Where are they?'

MacAlistair knew she meant Keach's army. 'Over in the 9th District, near the hospitals.'

The golden eyes, flecked with amber, told him that he'd better not be lying. She opened the door, and he went out to the rented car. The snow had paused for a moment, but the sky was leaden and low, and lights were already switched on in all the nearby shops. He cleared the white windows of the BMW; then got into it, sat there hunched into his warm coat, thinking about his friend in that hot office, thinking, 'Well, he had it coming to him and now he's got it.'

Catherine and David stared at the man who could have

been Alex Hunter's German brother, not with
amazement, because even MacAlistair's fairy-story had
prepared them for some change in him, but with
incomprehension. They had been able to accept him in
the well-worn role of failed businessman rescuing himself
and his family by means of crooked dealing, but now he
had told them that this was a pack of lies: that he had
never been a businessman at all and neither had
MacAlistair, that Artifax Ltd (and Inc.) around which
their lives had revolved was not a real business but a
front, that for all these years he had been—what?—some
kind of secret agent. He had told them that everything
which had seemed false, or at least suspect, such as his
endless absences, was the reality.

Catherine sat down, so disoriented that she felt
physically dizzy. David moved to her, touching her as if to
claim that he at least existed and was not about to turn
into a white rabbit. He himself was shocked by these
further revelations, but not surprised; long ago, unknown
to his mother, he had slipped through the Looking-Glass,
and all the things his father was saying, even the way he
looked, were simply extensions of the experience. Here in
this airless room his many suspicions made absolute sense;
cause and effect, so long disconnected, were at last in
accord. Once, walking along Piccadilly, he had been
afraid that the Looking-Glass world and the real world
were slowly becoming one; not it had happened, fusion
had taken place, and the result, though painful, was at
least real, even if 'reality' would never have the same
meaning again. The howling chaos outside the vacuum of
ordinary life was here and now, they were living in it,
perhaps they always had.

'You mean,' his mother was saying, 'that all those
business trips, Hong Kong, Greece, the States . . .'

'I came here, always here.'

She nodded to herself. Once or twice, on his returning,

she had noticed that his hair was shorter, though never this colour; he had excused it by saying that he had gone to the wrong barber in Istanbul or Calcutta, or wherever it was that he hadn't been. David was remembering the letter he had written to his father in Houston which had been answered by MacAlistair. He said, 'Patrick did the travelling.'

'Yes. He was Artifax, but he was much more than that. He was my cover, my contact, the only person in the world I dared trust. Sometimes he was actually me. We were . . . yes, two parts of the same man. Interdependent. Entirely.'

'Right from the beginning.' She said it as a statement, not a question. 'Before we were married.'

'Yes. I . . . can't ask you to forgive that. Perhaps I shouldn't have done it, Mac was always telling me I shouldn't have done it, he despised . . . despises me. But you were all I really had, all of you, you were real.'

'Real!' Her bitterness struck at him.

Renata came in with coffee and Schnapps; put the tray on the desk. Harshly, Catherine said, 'And this woman? I'd always guessed there was a woman.'

Renata straightened up; she didn't look ashamed, there was no cause for shame, and anyway it wasn't part of her nature. Alex Hunter said, 'Without Renata I couldn't have operated, I couldn't have existed.'

Catherine put a hand over her eyes, elbow on the table.

'And without you,' Renata added, 'he couldn't have existed either.' She went out of the room.

David could dimly discern through the prisms of this corridor of mirrors that there was a kind of reality here too, and he was old enough to know that the conversation was better wrenched away from such depths. 'But why did you have to . . . to drown, to disappear?'

His father shot him a grateful look; he ignored it.

'You have to understand my work here. It's . . . Nobody

knows about it, I suppose you'd be wise not to say anything—for your own good, not mine, they won't be able to touch me.' He went on to explain how, many years ago, it had been decided in the inner chambers of Western political power that whereas the Communists never ceased to subvert the Western countries, organizing strikes, inciting and arming dissatisfied minorities, infiltrating Trade Unions, stirring up ethnic fermentations, aggravating student unrest, the democracies had never taken this kind of warfare behind the frontiers of the Eastern bloc; and yet, witness events in all the subject Slav countries, not to mention within the USSR itself, the raw material was there.

And so 'Operation Resistance' had come into being. Professional agitators had been introduced into the Communist-controlled states, offering information, radio-links, training, arms. The response had been overwhelming. Within five years the whole conception needed to be reconsidered, reorganized, redoubled, rechristened: 'Group R'. Now it had a hand in every uprising, every 'incident', every act of defiance within the Russian-dominated territories.

Naturally, very little of this undercover rebellion was reported in the subject countries, let alone outside them. But the Russians knew; and they knew that there was a small but virulent secret army, guerrilla was too prosaic a name for it, able to sabotage military installations, annihilate tanks, poison water supplies, destroy aircraft with the most sophisticated weapons. Of course many brave men and women had been caught and killed, but such was the fury within these countries that a dozen volunteers came forward to take the place of every casualty.

'That's where I've been,' Alex Hunter told his staring wife and son. 'Not here, don't think I've been sitting here all these months, years.'

'Behind . . . behind the Iron Curtain?' Catherine was impressed in spite of herself, but then she had never seen this aspect of the man who had been her husband for two whole decades.

'Iron Curtain! It's rabbit-wire, rusted, full of holes.'

'And you've been behind it.'

'I live behind it. Well, half of me does, under other names, of course. And it's all beginning to work, to bear fruit, you can tell that even from the media in the West.' He was trying to curb his enthusiasm for fear of hurting them even more, for fear of revealing how vital to his very existence these activities had become; but the enthusiasm shone through, and even if they resented it there was no denying its potency.

'But why,' David persisted, 'did you have to drown and disappear?'

His father seemed to sag, some of the fire and certainty going out of him; he sat on the edge of the desk. 'Stupid. Stupid and simple.' He shook his head and sighed. 'One of the men I work with is called Jan Veretka, he's a Czech, he's . . . a wonderful man, dedicated, fearless, kind, funny. Possibly the finest, the *best* person I've ever known.

'Six months ago he was caught by the secret police, handed over to the Russians. He disappeared and we thought he was dead. Then, about five weeks ago, he came back. I won't tell you what they'd done to him. Bestial . . .' He put both hands over his face and pulled them downwards, as if trying to wipe away the memory. 'No, not bestial, beasts are merciful in their way. He'd been tortured, of course, battered until he was barely recognizable, broken to pieces really, he could just about walk. But the incredible thing was that they hadn't reached his mind, soul, call it what you like. That was indestructible.'

Horrified, Catherine said, 'Why? I mean, why did they

release him? As an example?'

He looked at her with sudden interest, as if her understanding came as a shock to him. 'Yes, as an example. And it certainly terrified a few people, among them my . . . superiors in Washington and London. It wasn't that they couldn't recognize his bravery, that was obvious enough, even to them.

'If he'd been captured, tortured and killed they could have accepted it; but he'd been captured, tortured and *released*, therefore he was a risk. It didn't really matter whether they'd brainwashed him, turned him into a double agent, or not. They hadn't, as it happens, you couldn't brainwash that man. No, it didn't matter; to them he was a number, a cog in the machine. They told me to kill him. But you see, to me he was a man.'

Catherine and David, faced with this husband and father they'd never known, could both guess the rest of the story.

'Of course I couldn't, wouldn't do it. Jesus Christ, if you'd *seen* him! To go through all that at the hands of your enemies and then get killed by your friends!' He shook his head violently. 'In any case I loved him, everybody did. And they're clever, we've trained them to be clever; if he'd suddenly disappeard they'd have known at once, and we'd have lost a thousand friends — more. That kind of news travels fast, the whole structure could have collapsed, and it would have served us right.'

Catherine sighed; looked down at her fur hat and her fine coat; stroked them absently as if to reassure herself that some other, less violent world did indeed exist. 'You disobeyed your orders.'

'Yes. I told Jan to hide, I gave him the money and the means. My bosses only found out a week after we'd gone to Tenerife. I knew that they'd send somebody to kill me; I mean, that was a foregone conclusion. Why not? From their point of view I was a worse risk than the man I'd saved. *And* a traitor! MacAlistair helped me, warned me . . .' He gestured. They knew the rest.

Catherine Hunter could not at first understand why she was accepting any of this, why she hadn't long before thrown herself at him, clawing the face which was so nearly the face she had once loved. The understanding, which came to her gradually, seemed to be upside down, but then so was reality. She had hated him for his absences, even wishing him dead; and when she had thought him to *be* dead, she had wanted him back in order to confess a tiny sexual dishonesty which haunted her conscience; but none of this was real and none of it mattered. The reality was very different, and extra-ordinary: she accepted him because she was a Matheson. This kind of behaviour, heroics, idealism and all, echoed back through the history of her family in every kind of dangerous situation which the world, including the British, had now forgotten — and they were feeling the loss. India, China, Africa, forgotten frontiers where men like Alex Hunter had nurtured duties and ideals, often mistaken no doubt, but still duties and ideals for which they were prepared to die. At one point in this strange meeting she had thought, 'I'll never forgive you for this,' but now she understood that it was the businessman she would have been unable to forgive, not the soldier; her mother, her great-grandmother had lived with just such men, with just such absences. If only he had been able to tell her the truth.

Even this musty shop made sense, the sallow man keeping watch, the woman who had been her husband's fellow-worker and occasional bedfellow, dusting books and keeping watch. She didn't need to ask Alex what he intended to do now, but asked all the same because, once said, it would be final; unsaid, it would perhaps remain to torment her.

Her husband glanced away. 'I have to go. If I don't go

they'll find me and kill me, no doubt about that.'

'To your friends on the other side of the frontier?'

He nodded, and was aware of her eyes flickering for a second towards Renata in the shop. He answered the unasked question: 'No, she's staying here, we need her here.'

Renata and Josef were talking together quietly. Josef slipped out into the yard, past the Simca, past the willowy girl's pottery, into the side-street.

MacAlistair had not switched on the lights of the car; he sat there hunched into his coat, motionless except for an occasional glance at the time. Nearly 4.15. Early darkness under the leaden sky. Sudden flurries of snow, clearing, recommencing. At 4.05 he had seen two men enter the café on the other side of the street; they were now drinking coffee at a table near the window; one of them was Keach.

Since 4.0 p.m. his men had been sidling into their prearranged positions surrounding the bookshop: clever positions chosen by MacAlistair that morning. It was true that he didn't know all of Josef's lookout points, but his long experience as a field-man, coupled with Keach's organizational expertise and Lorenz's cold analysis of the situation, made it possible to guess more or less exactly where they'd be. The man on the roof of the building in which the bookshop was situated had been killed at 4.10, by Joanna: an easy shot for that artist no doubt, in spite of snow and fading light; he had fired from one of the bedroom windows of a small hotel across the street. The supposition had been that this man probably held the key position in Josef's network. Now, at 4.19 by MacAlistair's watch, the others might well be growing uneasy; one or two might even have guessed what was afoot, but it was a *fait accompli*, they could only issue useless warnings, useless and too late.

Joanna was still waiting behind the curtains of the hotel bedroom in case Alex Hunter should be so stupid as to make a dash for it, one shot from somewhere above being cleaner and more anonymous than any untidy shoot-out on the ground. Yes, MacAlistair had covered every conceivable contingency.

Why had he done it? He really didn't know which of a score of answers was the true one, or whether they were all part of a single answer. He was a professional. He considered idealists to be dangerous and destructive. He had spent his youth hiding from drunken parents. Because he had purposely demolished his own marriage he believed that Alex Hunter was a selfish sonofabitch who had no right to deceive and destroy his family. He wasn't a fighter. He wasn't a traitor. He was a hick American, uninvolved, a nothing, hollow — he was full of ice. He resented being taken for granted and used as an accomplice. He had seen to it, as instructed, that his skill and luck had not deserted him in Vienna. He loathed Alex Hunter, he loved him. Why had he done it?

4.20 — any moment now! For the last time he and Alex were working to the exact second.

Josef erupted into the bookshop from the yard, shaking with excitement and anger. 'They're here, they're all over the place. Oh Jesus, the bastard, the *bastard!*' He had spoken in Czech without knowing it. Renata spun round towards the office, but Alex Hunter had already heard. Shock electrified the confined space.

Catherine said, 'What is it?' David, so much older, already used to the Looking-Glass world, had guessed; and had also guessed that MacAlistair was responsible. Alex Hunter closed his eyes and stood stock-still, as if he had been shot but would not fall over. 'Oh God! I never . . . never for one moment thought . . .'

'You never thought! *I told you!*' The lioness had disguised herself out of deference to the wife; now she blazed. Catherine and David stared in astonishment.

'Not Mac!'

'You English, you are such *children*!' Perhaps this was an old jibe, in any event she must have known that it would smack some life back into him. Josef was moving towards the broom cupboard, but she snapped, 'No! MacAlistair will have told them.'

'The yard?' Hunter looked at Josef, but he was still dazed, seeming not to care.

'No, and not the roof; they killed Klaus.'

The seconds were ticking by. Outside in the BMW, MacAlistair again glanced at his watch. 4.20 exactly. Catherine Hunter and her son would come hurrying out of the shop at any second. The signal for which Keach and his men were waiting would be given by the car; as soon as it drove away the operation would leap forward to a quick and quiet conclusion.

Alex Hunter said, 'Take your Simca and make a dash for it?'

'You wouldn't get a hundred metres.'

Hunter nodded; glanced at his wife and son. 'I might do better to go quietly, I'm thinking of our friends on the other side.'

'Oh, for God's sake, Alex, they *need* you.' As she spoke her eye was caught by the wife's beautiful coat and fur hat.

MacAlistair started the car to make sure that it wasn't too cold; BMW's were infallible but nothing rented could ever be relied upon completely. 4.22. Snow was falling again; he cleared it with both front and rear wipers. It was sticking to the side-window—not much he could do about that; he rolled the window down, snow swept in, cold on his face; he rolled it up again, but visibility was still bad.

Now . . . Yes, the door of the shop was opening. And here they came, running, panic-stricken perhaps, the boy holding his mother's arm, both bending against wind-blown snow. He leaned across to open the rear door for Catherine; opened it; looked directly into the face of Alex Hunter wearing her fur hat, and knew that he was a dead man.

David was amazed at the quietness of the shot. He did exactly as he'd been told, pushed MacAlistair's sagging body straight across to the passenger seat and clambered in, squashed between the door as he slammed it and the dead man's hip, kicking the lifeless feet to one side. He was aware of his father reaching forward, heaving at MacAlistair's weight, but from behind and without being seen to make an enormous effort there was little he could do. He gripped the back of the overcoat collar and jerked the lolling head upright, holding it thus in some semblance of life. Meanwhile, thanks to MacAlistair's preparations, David had started the car at a touch, and, thanks to snow and fading light, the very factors upon which MacAlistair had relied to conceal his operation, Keach and the hidden men were unable to see exactly what was happening.

Now the car began to move. MacAlistair's head jerked back, Alex Hunter pushed it forward again; and the nearest of Keach's men, watching the car as it accelerated past his position some fifty yards down the Wiedner Hauptstrasse, only noticed that David Hunter and not MacAlistair was driving; MacAlistair seemed to be turning in the passenger seat to speak to Mrs Hunter behind him. Snow and falling darkness obscured the rest.

In any case the importance of MacAlistair and the BMW at this moment lay in the car moving away; the signal had been given. Keach and his companion hurried out of the café and ran across the street; eight other men were aleady converging on the bookshop. Both doors were locked, but it only took a few seconds to smash a glass pane at the front of the shop and break in. Four men, guns in hand, took the office with copybook precision, but were less certain what to do when they found standing inside it nothing but two defiant women.

9

David was driving as fast as he dared. For a mile, perhaps two, time and distance had no meaning, he followed his father's directions without thought: left — right — right at the next lights — get into the left lane . . . One of MacAlistair's legs kept intruding between his own foot and the accelerator. His scant experience of driving in England had accustomed him to the other side of the road, he was not used to heavy snow, and moreover the Viennese rush-hour, one of the more lethal in Europe, was just beginning. He was relieved beyond measure when his father said, 'I don't think we're being followed, God knows why not! Turn right and stop, we'll change places.

They did so at speed. Before taking the wheel, Alex Hunter opened the passenger door, pulled MacAlistair's legs away from the controls and pushed his body down on the floor. Since MacAlistair was a big man, the upper part of his torso still sprawled across the seat. His old friend threw his wife's luxurious coat over it, and slammed the door. A few seconds later they were again moving, the whole thing had taken less than a minute.

He now said to his son, 'Watch the road behind; if you even suspect anyone's following us tell me at once.' For this reason, David's later memory of the journey was confused by the fact that he had seen most of it backwards. He thought he recognized the Hofburg and the Ring, and he was right, but soon afterwards they swung off on to side-streets again, then on to faster, wider roads leading out of the city.

Up to this point they had hardly spoken at all. Now David said, 'Where are we going?'

'I'm going to Czechoslovakia. I'll drop you off in a few minutes. Got any money?'

'Yes.' He turned then from his scrutiny of the road behind them and looked at his father, frowning. 'Will you be all right?'

'As all right as I ever have been.' He glanced in the mirror. 'Watch the road, Davey. What I mean by that is, I haven't been much use to you, any of you.'

'I suppose everybody gets by as best they can.'

'That sounds old.'

'I'm not as young as I was.'

Hunter glanced in the mirror again, hoping to see the expression on the loved face, but it was turned from him, doing its duty. The voice said, 'I found your glasses.'

'My . . . ?'

'In Tenerife. Your reading glasses. What happened?'

'I dropped them. I was in a hurry.'

'All smashed up.'

'Well, they were a dead giveaway, weren't they? I didn't do a very good job, I needed that tide.'

'To carry you round the Point. Quite a swim!'

'The alternative was a bullet.'

David knew about the bullet too; he wondered what the range had been to his beer-mug. That preoccupation with the glasses seemed to lie far away now, in another time and place to which he could never return. Yet they had been the first thing, the first question, the first step into this unknown country.

They were crossing water, the Danube, all but invisible in a fresh flurry of snow. Alex Hunter said, 'You can relax. If they haven't got us by now they're not on to us, but take an occasional look, just in case.' This time, even though his son had turned, he couldn't really discern his features because the street-lamps were more infrequent, the snow heavier. 'We won't be seeing each other again, Davey. Try not to think too badly of me.'

David found it difficult to think of him at all; he had split up into dozens of different men, some receding, some approaching, some alive, some dead. He supposed that one day this diversified man would recompose himself into a single recognizable figure. Or he might not. Either way, it seemed that the Looking-Glass world was here to stay.

The city was behind them now, dwindling to a few scattered lights, dimly seen. Alex Hunter said, 'I suppose Mac was right, I screwed it all up, most people do. I mean you, your mother, Annie. It isn't that the other thing became more important . . .' He didn't finish the sentence. David, a witness to the inner fire that had blazed out of him when he had spoken of 'the other thing', guessed that in a way it always *had* been more important.

Lights loomed up: a café in the middle of a snowfield; even the road was becoming difficult to define. Alex Hunter stopped the car and turned to his son. 'Try to look after your mother. I don't mean financially, she's all right financially, I mean . . . I loved her, I really did.'

David nodded. The 'other thing' was there again, and he didn't understand it, doubted whether he ever would. His father put out an arm and they embraced clumsily, the back of the driving-seat between them; many things between them. 'Give my love to Annie. And think of me, Davey. I shall always think of you, all of you.'

The coat had slipped away, revealing one of MacAlistair's hands; they both looked at it, pale in the wavering light from the café. Alex Hunter said, 'Poor Mac, I expected too much of him.' He reached out and adjusted the coat to hide the hand; it was a strangely tender gesture, but might just as well have been mere expediency. In a flash of insight David thought that it probably symbolized his father's entire life.

He got out of the car and watched it drive away into whirling snow.

In the bookshop, Catherine Hunter and Renata were now alone together; the bully-boys had searched the place from top to bottom, tearing much of it apart, before withdrawing, truculent or shamefaced, and empty-handed.

Catherine, unused to them, found that she was trembling; Renata, who had lived with them all her life, noted this with wonder and then compassion; she poured out massive doses of Schnapps. As they lifted the glasses, shaking hand and firm hand, the same thought crossed both their minds; their eyes met, cool grey eyes from the lush meadows of England, flaming golden eyes from the battlefield of central Europe. In the end they didn't drink to Alex Hunter, who needed neither of them, or who needed both of them, they would never know which; they drank, privately, to themselves and perhaps to each other.

David Hunter lost sight of the red tail-lights of the car; peered a little longer; then turned into the café which, surprisingly, greeted him with a burst of music and laughter. He ordered a beer in his faulty German and asked how he could get back to Vienna. There would be a bus, the landlord told him, in twenty minutes. Snow? No, this was nothing!

A pretty, plump girl who waited on the tables said something he couldn't understand, laughing. The landlord translated: 'She says that if the bus doesn't come she knows of a bed you can share.' There was more laughter — pretty girl, handsome boy — red country faces splitting into jollity. Life went on, bursting at the seams.

*

Five miles away, Alex Hunter drove as near as he dared to the edge of the road and stopped. He made sure that no cars were approaching; then stumbled round to the passenger door, opened it, heaved out his friend's body. He dragged it to the lee of a clump of bushes, every branch thickly white, glittering in the reflected glow of the headlights. Immediately, gently, the snow began to cover it. Alex Hunter returned to the car and drove on towards another frontier.